Darkness Beyond the Night

Darkness Beyond the Night

Brenda Joyce Fay

Order this book online at www.trafford.com
or email orders@trafford.com

Most Trafford titles are also available at major online book retailers.

Printed in the United States of America.

ISBN: 978-1-4269-9457-9 (sc)
ISBN: 978-1-4269-9458-6 (e)

Library of Congress Control Number: 2011916088

Trafford rev.09/07/2011

 www.trafford.com

North America & International
toll-free: 1 888 232 4444 (USA & Canada)
phone: 250 383 6864 ♦ fax: 812 355 4082

In memory of my beloved parents,

And

Dedicated to my husband and my children …

Without them, this book would not have been possible.

CONTENTS

Chapter 1

The Journey Begins

The year is 2009. The month is April. The scene depicts a spine chilling image in Catherine's mind. She sees a dark shadow passing from behind her ... she feels a cold wet cloth over her mouth ... there's an awful smell and the sound of a man's voice that she will never forget. What does it all mean? The scene repeats itself over and over, haunting her for the past seventeen years. Weeks of her life disappeared. She longs for the day when she knows what happened in the *darkness beyond the night?* Join me in her journey.

Catherine is a young, gentle soul of twenty-two. She's about 5 feet 7 inches tall with medium blond silky hair that drapes beautifully in waves, almost to her waist. Her eyes are as green and as captivating as emeralds with long, brown eye lashes. Her complexion is pale, smooth and flawless. Unbeknown to most, she, like her father, brother, and grandfather, has a cute little dimple in both of her shoulders. She thrives on *living life to its fullest.* She is spontaneous and acts instinctively ... one never knows what she will be doing from one minute to the next. Spontaneity is only one of her great qualities. She has a brilliant mind, broad intuition, and a wit that keeps everyone laughing. Her desire, motivation, and ability to accomplish whatever she undertakes are outstanding. In relationships, she is the truest of friends as long as others are true to her; otherwise she's a bit of the tiger. She's versatile in different or difficult situations, which allows her to be successful in whatever she does. She has little difficulty in attracting others, in fun or at work. Her willingness to accommodate attracts many significant others, but something festering inside her keeps her at arm's reach. Her devotion to family may be her best attribute or her worst, and at times it will be hard to tell which. She can do just about anything as long as she's free to be creative. If not, she is prone to depression and doesn't know why. Once when she was in one of her depressed moods, her grandfather quoted Henry David Thoreau, saying: "The mass of men lead lives of quiet desperation." He continued, "Now Catherine, pull yourself up by your boot straps and stop this nonsense ... the good Lord helps those who help themselves. Think of something more positive and enjoyable, and move on."

Catherine lives with Grandmother Alice whom she adores and in whose presence she always feels safe. She has been the only stable force in Catherine's life. Alice often says that being a grandmother brings meaning to her life. To her, being a grandparent seems to outweigh any burden. With today's families being constantly on the move, having a history that bonds them together is difficult. Grandmother Alice brings that bond to this family. At sixty-eight she is still lovely and distinguished, with long, softly curled silver hair, sky blue eyes and a beautiful smile. She gets up every morning at 5:30 am, puts on a fresh pressed top and slacks, makes sure her hair is styled smoothly on top of her head and readies herself for the day. She is always neat, clean, and smells of her favorite perfume, *White Diamonds*. She's always courteous and pleasant, and seems to know just what to say no matter what the occasion, to make someone feel comfortable and at ease. She is a beautiful, energetic soul who has devoted her life to caring for others. Whether gardening, cleaning, doing laundry, or cooking, she seems tireless.   Having raised three sons and two daughters through some happy and some very difficult, almost unbelievable situations, it seems as though she could handle almost anything.   She lost Grandfather Edwin very suddenly two years ago and had to learn the lessons of bitter grief and loss, alone.   They had been married for fifty years and were knit closely together as one soul.   The loss of her husband was almost more than she could bear. Catherine was there for her, but couldn't lessen the pain and grief of her loss.   Only time has allowed her to recover.   Now, her life centers on Catherine.

Catherine and Alice live in Vestal Center.   It's a very small township located at the intersection of NY-26 and County road 53, on the *Big Choconut Creek*.   That's about four miles south of the main district of Vestal.   A peaceful stream runs behind a tree line close to their home and at night Catherine can feel the chilly breeze coming off the water.   The crickets chirp incessantly and the frogs croak their song as she walks along the bank.   She finds solace here as she wonders and questions, three weeks of my life are blocked out of my memory, why?

The name Vestal comes from the *Vestal Virgins* of Ancient Rome.   They were holy priestesses of Vesta, the Goddess of the Hearth.   They were the only female priests within the Roman religious system.   Committed at a young age, usually between six and ten years of age, they were sworn to celibacy for a period of 30 years, ten as students, ten in service, and ten as teachers. Afterwards, they could marry if they chose to do so.   However, few took the opportunity to leave their respected role.   To do so would require them to submit to the authority of a man. Catherine, for the past several years has felt a special connection with these women.   She, a young virgin herself, wishes to remain celibate out of fear, a fear from deep within tied to the awful night that haunts her. In all of her twenty-two years she has never dated. Many young men have asked her out, but she refused.   When Grandma Alice asked her why she doesn't date, Catherine said, "I have more important things to do with my time." Unwilling to push too much, Grandmother Alice hopes Catherine will change her mind soon.

The white, clapboard farm house where they live was built in the early 1940's by a prominent carpenter of the time named Edward Eugene Taylor, Catherine's great-grandfather.   It sits in a little secluded valley, just two miles Southwest of Vestal Center. Nestled in the center of four huge Maple trees, it resembles a *Courier and Ives* painting. There's an old wishing well in the front yard with a bucket that you can raise and lower for water, but it hasn't been used in years.   Now, the well is capped off and the bucket is full of beautiful purple, blue and pink petunias. There's a big red barn at the back of the property, and at the end of the driveway. Behind the barn is twenty acres of wooded area, pine trees, a small fishing pond and a logging road that circles through the property and leads out to the main road from behind the barn. Years ago, Edward, his son Edwin and his grandson Ted used to hunt white-tail deer there during hunting season. Edwin's wife Alice now leases the property to a hunting club during the fall and winter hunting season.

The barn has two large doors that slide together in the front. Above them is a hayloft with a window that opens to the front. A dirt driveway leads from the doors along the left side of the house and out to the main road. The barn used to house Snowflake, five other horses and two milk cows. Over the years, Grandfather sold the other horses and cows and just kept Snowflake. She was a lovely, gentle Morgan horse with a very sweet nature. She stood about 15.2 hands high (each hand equals 4 inches in height). Her coat was a beautiful caramel and white color. When she looked at you with her large brown eyes, you couldn't help but want to give her a big hug. When you rode her she moved with a spring in her step. What a great horse. Now without her, the barn just houses a wagon, farming equipment, and a truck during the winter. Catherine and Alice never go near the barn any more.

The house is surrounded by a covered porch in the front and half-way down both sides. About ten feet to the left of the big double doors in the front hangs an old wooden swing that Grandfather Edwin made special for Catherine. He used to sit next to her on it and read stories to her while Grandmother Alice fixed the evening meal. To the right of the front doors is a cane rocking chair that Grandmother Alice still spends a great deal of time in. She likes to sit in it in the cool of the evening, wrap up in her favorite throw with a cup of hot Chamomile Lemon tea, and read.

On each side of the front doors is a tall, beautifully colored, stained glass window depicting angels surrounded by light, brightly colored hummingbirds and pink roses. Above the door there is a half-moon shaped stained glass window with a white dove in the center. On each side of the dove are white and pink dogwood blossoms. The doors lead into a foyer with a polished oak wooden floor, and a small oval carpet to wipe your feet on. In the corner stands a coat rack where Ted, Alice's son, used to hang his hat and jacket. His hat still hangs on it. Grandmother Alice can't bear to part with it. To the left of the foyer is the living room where a fire still burns in the fireplace on cold winter nights. The floor in the living room is wooden with an oriental carpet covering the sitting area in front of the fire-place. The furniture consists of a davenport on the left side of the fire-place and two over-stuffed colonial chairs on the right side with a lamp stand between them. The upholstery has pink and blue colored flowers on a background of cream and beige. There are also two mahogany chairs with a table between them just to the right as you enter the room. On top of the fire-place is a heavy wooden mantle with a large Victorian mirror hanging above it. On the mantle, family pictures are arranged four on each side of a beautiful porcelain vase. It's filled with peach colored roses from Alice's garden. Six of the pictures are of Catherine's family - her mother Joyce, her father Ted, her brother Chris, her

Grandmother Alice, and her Grandfather Edwin. There is one picture there of all of them together, when Catherine was just a little girl of four. It was taken at Christmas time seventeen years ago, a much happier time. The other two are of Grandmother Alice's other children and grandchildren. Besides Ted she had two more boys and two girls.

At the end of the foyer is a winding staircase that leads up to five bedrooms and two bathrooms. The two bedrooms in the back are closed off now and no-one goes in them. It is said, that you can hear cries and voices coming from one of them on a cold winter night. The other three bedrooms are Catherine's, Grandmother Alice's and the third is a guest bedroom.

Beyond the foyer downstairs there's a dining room on the left and the kitchen on the right. A pantry, half-bath and a mud room are behind the dining room and kitchen. The mud room just recently was converted into a laundry room to make life easier for Grandmother Alice, since it is quite difficult for her to go up and down the steep, narrow stairs to the basement. The basement is mostly used for storage now. Ted and Joyce had wanted to make it into a recreation room for when the children were older, but with everything that happened, Grandmother Alice could not afford to do it.

To the right of the foyer is the library. Shelves in the back and on both sides are full of books that Catherine and Alice love to read. Just to the left as you enter the room are two soft, over stuffed, comfortable reading chairs on either side of a table with a light on it. In the middle of the room is a shiny black *Baby Grand* piano with the top up. Catherine took piano lessons on it, starting on her sixth birthday. She now spends several hours a week playing classical, soft rock, country, and religious music on it. Her favorite composer is Georg Bohm (1661-1733), one of the leading organists and composers in Thuringia, Germany. He exercised a strong influence on Bach. Although he wrote numerous cantatas and sacred songs, he is remembered more for his keyboard works. Catherine's favorite piece is called *Chorale Partite*. She likes the organ too, but the piano is still her favorite musical instrument. Though unusual for most pianists, Catherine loves to play musical combinations by picking parts of her favorite pieces and playing them one after the other. When she plays, Alice will often come in and listen, letting her mind wander back to times when her daughter-in-law, Joyce, would play.

This morning is bright and cheerful as the sun streams through the stain-glassed window in the front of the Library dispersing a rainbow of sparkling colors, across the piano ... so very peaceful. Above the window, carved in an arch, we see four triangles symbolic of the four elements: water, fire, earth, and air; they are also symbols for the four seasons: spring, summer, fall and winter. Fine details of angels are also depicted in the oak woodwork throughout the library, foyer, dining room, and living room, typical of the delicate hand-crafted symmetrical work of Catherine's great-grandfather.

The four elements were significant to Edward. Though he was only part Iroquois, the elements were a big part of his Indian culture and very significant even today. According to Empedocles, a Greek philosopher, scientist and healer who lived in Sicily in the fifth century B.C., all matter is comprised of them. Developed by him and expanded by Aristotle, these four elements are not only material substances, but are also spiritual essences. The interaction of the four elements is influenced by the relationship between the *two great life energies of Love, associated with Good, and Strife associated with evil.* From the standpoint of Carl Jung's psychology, these are also facets of our personality and our psyche; present in all people as intuition, sensation, thinking and feeling. They, along with our four seasons of life significantly influence many of our cultural traditions today. When Great-Grandfather Edward carved them into the woodwork, it took him back to his Iroquois Indian traditions. His grandfather was half Iroquois and lived with the Iroquois tribe just outside of Syracuse, NY. He could not have known their significance on his progeny. Or, could he have felt that the elements and seasons would affect all life and death, including theirs'?

As the sun is rising in the East we can see Catherine swinging on the swing as she does most every morning and often in the evening after dinner. The air is fresh this morning with a slight breeze bringing the sweet scent of lilacs to her from the bushes on the either side of the porch. Catherine loves the lilacs. Like her father, she sometimes places one on her pillow at night. The scent seems to relax her as she passes off to sleep. Early spring is her favorite time of year, though she also loves the bright colors of the changing leaves in the fall and the first gentle snow of winter. She likes to bring a cup of hot chocolate out with her when she swings ... and dreams of what her life would be like if things were different. Oh how she wishes her life was different. There's a feeling of emptiness she can't describe. She turned twenty-two, January 19th, and since then has become quite withdrawn and pensive.

She awoke this morning just as she always does in her home in Vestal Center. She has lived here all twenty-two years of her life, but only fifteen with both of her grandparents, and only the last two with just Grandmother Alice. Her grandfather died two years ago. No one else is in the house but Alice, who is fixing breakfast in the kitchen as she does every morning for Catherine.

Like Catherine, Alice is a very generous spirit; she would do most anything for someone she loves. There are some things however that she just cannot do. She knows how much Catherine wants to know about the loss of her parents and brother, but she doesn't know the exact circumstances surrounding Joyce's death and doesn't know what happened to Ted. It's so very painful for her to think about it so she doesn't discuss it with Catherine. Through life insurance and retirement investments, Ted and Edwin left Alice and Catherine with enough money for them to live comfortably. Alice hired a handy-man to come over on a regular basis to make repairs and keep the property in good condition. There are other homes nearby, but they are quite a distance away, one to the North and one to the South. Too far for anyone to hear or see anything that happens at the farm. It's a very quiet neighborhood most of the time, very serene and peaceful. Almost too quiet... the atmosphere is suspenseful and foreboding at times especially in the late evening.

Alice experiences fear at times, just as Catherine does. Today as Alice listens to the news she hears as we all do... that humanity is headed for extinction ... that our society is falling apart as a result of apathy for others and our selfish narcissism. The news today reported a shooting of a sixteen year old boy in a drug deal gone badly. It instantly put Alice into a reflective state. She relives, daily, the pain of losing her son and daughter-in-law to violence. The sadness consumes her ... the thought of young innocent lives wasted uselessly. The negatives that surround her life and those of every family, so contrary to the older generations are seemingly now the norm for society. There is so much contempt, and malice shown for others, so much violence. Alice has seen it first hand and having lost so very much, she questions whether society can possibly heal itself, or has it gone too far?

Alice wants to be forgiving, but finds it extremely difficult. Every Sunday, she dresses in her finest dress, stockings and high-heels and goes off to church. She hears the words that we are to live by and does her very best, but the pain in her heart never seems to diminish. The strife, poverty, despairs, and loss of hope for so many brings tears to her eyes. She worries ... what's in store for her children and grandchildren? She's gone through so much herself and has been told to be brave, that God is by her side to help her. She knows she needs to be strong for Catherine

… that Grandmothers are supposed to be uniquely appointed to have the answers to life's questions, but when Catherine asks her why life is so disturbing and violent, she has no recourse but to say she doesn't know why. She tells Catherine "That everyone makes their own destiny, that it's not a matter of chance, it's a matter of choice … a thing we must achieve." What's our ultimate purpose she wonders? Usually, when Catherine comes to her with problems, she would remember similar situations from her past. Situations that Joyce and Ted had experienced and how they resolved them. By relating these to Catherine, she hopes to answer some of Catherine's questions and hopes it will allow her to discover a little of what her parents were like.

Memories came flooding back to Alice as she thought of her son and daughter-in-law. Joyce seemed more like a daughter to her than a daughter-in-law. She was always so considerate and loving towards Alice. She was a vivacious, distinguished lady with long medium blonde hair and deep, emerald green eyes like Catherine's. Her features were very delicate, yet striking. She was so graceful, warm and charming even under the worst of circumstances. Alice said that Catherine and Joyce were very much alike, the image of each other. Joyce taught Behavioral Sciences at the State University in Vestal[1] for almost twelve years. She loved to teach and had a depth of understanding for young people that amazed her colleagues. Her communication skills made every student feel important, that each was equally worthy of her attention. She felt that challenging the developing mind of each student could bring forth great truths …that every student had something to offer if they would just dig deep into their heart and mind. They needed to be critical of what they read and heard. However, they needed to do research and prove the truth … not to just believe literally, everything said or written in textbooks and literature, or on-line. She always said, "The questioning mind leads to wisdom and that reason is the wise man's guide." (possibly a quote from Socrates). Joyce put her whole heart into teaching and the students loved her for it. It was said, that she spent more time on lesson plans and research than she did in the classroom, which was true. She could have achieved so much more had her life not been cut short. Her life short lived ... was not fair to her.

Alice's son, Ted, was about 6 feet 2 inches tall, a lanky man with broad shoulders. His face was stern with high cheek bones, a tanned complexion and hazel eyes. His black hair surrounding his face, curled gently around his ears. He was a staunch individual who conducted himself with confidence and somberness unexpected of men of his stature. He was a devoted family man who loved his wife and children deeply and would do anything to keep them safe and to see them happy. He felt richly blessed to have them. He was so excited when Joyce gave birth to Christopher. Now he thought I have the perfect family, a beautiful little girl and a healthy baby boy. He looked forward to the day when he could play ball with Chris and take long walks with him like he did with Catherine. They would walk along the banks of the stream nearby and skip rocks across the water. Catherine was the *apple of his eye*. She was always such a cheerful little one, skipping and walking along beside him. While they walked they would sing songs together and he would tell her stories. He would come home from a rough day at work, all it would take would be a smile from her and "Hi daddy," and Ted would be happy. "All was not happy though."

Something about work seemed to bother him more frequently. The past ten years, he worked in sales for IBM, commonly called *Big Blue*, in Endicott and traveled at least two weeks out of every month. It was hard being away from the family, but he had no choice. It was in the last few years that he seemed to be more troubled than usual. Sales were down and money was tight, but the bills got paid. He never complained and always felt that in everything the middle course was best, that all things in excess brought trouble. To that extent he was very conservative and left nothing to chance. He always planned more for the future, saying "Today would take care of itself." Because work was slow he got worried and withdrew some of his retirement to invest in something ... he didn't say what. The important thing was that Joyce and the family knew the investment had been a success.

One night a couple of weeks after he made his big investment, Ted called and said he couldn't make it back home that night, but he'd be back in a day or two. No questions were asked, since he often worked out of town. Two days later, when he returned home, he seemed to be even more troubled than usual, like the weight of the world was upon his shoulders. Joyce met him at the door and could sense something was drastically wrong. She yearned to help him, but he pushed past her and said, "Please, just leave me alone." Joyce had seen that look before, and knew to leave him alone. When he felt this way he would just shut down. After a hot shower and a long talk to someone on the telephone, he came back downstairs, very pensive and quiet. At times like these he would fix himself a stiff drink, sit for a few minutes and then go into the library and play his violin until a peaceful relaxation came over him. You could tell, he would begin by drawing the bow across the strings with quick firm strokes and as he continued ... soon the strokes would become more graceful and he would pluck the strings more gently. We knew then he had relaxed. He played the violin superbly. He was often asked to play it in church on Sunday or at special functions. When he played it was like he was in his own little world, oblivious to his surroundings.

Grandmother Alice, Grandfather Edwin, Joyce, Ted and the two children all lived together until January of that fateful year, then life as they knew it changed forever.

Chapter 2

My Father, My Friend

My father, Ted Murphy, was born May 17, 1960. He was the youngest one of five children, three boys and two girls. He was raised by his father, my grandfather, Edwin Eugene Murphy, and his mother, my grandmother, Alice Elizabeth Murphy. The rest of the children had left home before I was born. Growing up they all lived in the same house that I was raised in, in Vestal Center. Their lives were fairly simple; centered around home, school, and church. The township was small enough that everyone knew everyone and all helped each other out in times of need. Many considered people living in this tight knit community to be *country bumpkins*. It was true, where we lived was definitely simple country living compared to Vestal four miles away, but not very rustic. Living on the farm as my family did, they would be considered to be quite *well off*. *Well off* being subjective of course. The family wealth amounted to a Belgium draft work horse named Dusty, a Morgan horse named Snowflake, three quarter horses named Max, Sunshine, and Betsey and two milk cows, Daisy and Marshmallow. The house built in the 40's by my dad's grandfather Edward was situated on 21 acres of land, 20 acres behind the barn with a 10 acre fishing pond surrounded by pine trees. Most of the farms in the area could claim a similar degree of wealth. They were all about the same size and all had gardens and fruit trees just as my grandparents did.

Most of what I know about my father came from tales that my grandparents told me. He was an adorable baby and an even cuter little boy with black hair that curled softly around his ears. Grandmother Alice would pull out all pictures she had of him and show them to me from *time- to-time*. She said, "He was always so happy. His hazel eyes just glistened with excitement as a little boy. Though very sweet, he would get into all kinds of trouble at home just like any little boy. That was ok though because when we went out to church or to friend's houses, etc. he was as *good as gold*. At home he felt comfortable to *raise cane* with his brothers and sisters and *cut loose* as the all did." She saved all of his report cards. As I expected, he was an exemplary student, he liked math and science the most, but he excelled at everything.

Grandmother Alice told me a cute little story about my father when he was eleven years old. "He fancied this girl in his class, named Rebecca. He would walk a mile out of his way to go by her house so he could walk to school with her. He even carried her books. He would get up twenty minutes early and rush through breakfast so he would have more time to get to her house. When anyone asked him about her he would be so embarrassed, his face would get bright red. Regrettably for him, it didn't last long. Three months later the family moved away."

My father made friends easily in school, but didn't join in sports or socialize with them after school. He spent most of his time helping Grandfather Edwin with chores and working around the farm. He enjoyed learning carpentry, farming and gardening from his grandfather. He was a great problem solver, very logic oriented. Whenever anyone said they needed help or couldn't fix something, he was the first one to offer help. There was a warmer side to him too. He loved the animals and always showed a great deal of compassion for others. He was always very respectful to others.

Following high-school, my father attended Broome Community College in Binghamton where he earned an AA degree in Electrical Technology. He then went to the State University of NY in Vestal where he met my mother, Joyce Marie Baker. They both earned Bachelor Degrees in Liberal Arts with honors and decided to continue two more years to get their Master's Degrees. Dad earned his in Languages and mom earned hers in Behavioral Sciences.

Grandmother Alice said, "Dad and mom were very much *in love*, but didn't feel they were ready to be married. Dad had entered the ROTC program at the University so once he completed his education he went directly into the Marine's. In the fall of 1981 mom started teaching Psychology classes at the State University of NY in Binghamton.

Eight years later, after 2 tours of duty in Bosnia, he came home and proposed to mom. Six months later they married, and one year later I was born. Looking at his military picture, I see a very confident, strong, very masculine individual. He was very handsome. I definitely see why my mother was attracted to him. The attributes that you can't see in that picture, are his warmth and loving ways he shared with me in the five years that I knew him. I cherish the moments that we shared. I still remember his strength when he held my hand as we walked together, when he cradled me in his arms, when he twirled me around as we played in the yard, and when he comforted me when I had nightmares. The times we spent together were so special to me; I hold them close to my heart.

Fortunately for me, Grandfather Edwin carried on where my dad left off. We spent a lot of time together. He often compared me to my father. He once said, "You're a chip off the old block, so much like your dad. You have his strength, his courage, and his same quality of mind and spirit. These have enabled you to face the dangers, the pain and the sorrow that you've endured. You've been so brave; …definitely a survivor, but now you have your Grandmother and me to lean on."

Grandfather compared me to my mother too when he said, "Such a sweet young lady you've turned out to be. That comes from your mom. She was beautiful inside and out …in every way, just like you. When she and your dad first met, your dad said, 'We were instantly attracted to each other.' That's exactly how I felt about your Grandmother, *Love at first sight.*"

Grandfather liked to tell stories about my father when we sat on the porch swing. One went like this. "When your dad was just a little boy, about seven years old, you could see how confident and self-assured he was at trying new things, like riding his favorite horse, Sunshine, bareback, jumping ditches with his bicycle, or even entering writing and speech contests at school. He worked hard and studied hard. He was determined to succeed in everything he did. As the years passed, we also witnessed him grow in strength of character. He always took the moral high ground in his relationship with others; …in everything he did. I was always proud of him. He stepped in when he saw others being mistreated by bullies at school or on the playground. He joined the military because he had such a passion for standing up for others. I see those same strengths in you Catherine. I'm so very proud of you."

What I've learned most from listening to my Grandparent's tell their stories about my parents is that no problem is insurmountable. We have all the support and love from our family and all the faith we need to deal with whatever comes our way.

Chapter 3

Catherine's Memories

At twenty-two, Catherine's old enough, and it's time ... she's going to tell you her part of the story.

This morning as I sat on the swing sipping my hot-chocolate, a chilly breeze brought goose-bumps up on my arms. "I should be happy," I thought. I'm going to be graduating from SUNY, Binghamton soon. I have a good job and a possible great career ahead of me. I really have no worries. My grandmother takes great care of me but the problem is ... I'm not happy. I thought, "... what is wrong with me?" I have so many questions. I am so blessed and I have so much to be thankful for, why am I not content with my life? What happened to my parents and my brother? I miss them. Why did my grandparents have to raise me? There's this horrible feeling of emptiness in me that I can't describe. Please don't think I am ungrateful. I love Grandmother Alice and she has been wonderful to me, but she has never been willing to talk to me about what happened to my family. I suppose it is possible that she really doesn't know what happened. Well, enough of these unanswered questions. I need to put them aside for now, I don't want to be late for work.

I hastily got ready for work and as I pulled out of the driveway I felt like something was grabbing at my insides telling me that I must do something now. That it can't wait … so much so that it's made me nauseous. What couldn't wait? I debated calling in sick to work, but decided I would just have to work through it. I didn't know why, but for the last four months or so, I've been feeling very ill-at-ease. I have a lot of nervous energy and can't seem to stay put for any length of time. Grandmother Alice told me, "You are like a hummingbird - delicate and graceful, but fluttering all around. If you have to you can remain still for awhile, then you dart off and become as busy as a bee." Today, I feel more like that than usual. I can feel it. There's something out there that changes all of us from time-to-time … moves us and pushes us to do things that we didn't believe we could possibly do. Maybe for me it has to do with the *seasons of my life* that my father used to tell me about. Though I'm grown now and will soon graduate from college I don't know what to do with my life, maybe that's why the sick feeling in the pit of my stomach. I know I should be starting a career … and then again … maybe that's not it at all.

Every week-day morning for the past three years, I've been working part time as an assistant to the editor for the local newspaper, the *Evening Press*. After work, I rush to my classes in photography and journalism at the State University. With graduation coming soon I'm hoping to be hired on at the Press full-time. Graduation is the first week in May and yes, in just three weeks I will have my BA in Journalism. It seems as though I've been taking classes forever.

Today as I drove to work I thought, "If work is slow today I can do a little research and access some microfiche newspaper clippings for 'January 19, 1992' … the last time I remember seeing my parents and brother.

My research didn't happen. My boss came over to my desk shortly after I arrived at work and said, "I need you to *sweat bullets* for me today, Catherine. That story Brian gave us for the evening paper is a disaster." Yes Sir, I said. Oh well, I thought ... soon I will have time and I can find out something. Someone, something, somewhere has to have some answers for me.

New York just went onto daylight savings in April so tonight; I still have a couple of hours of daylight left after class. That will give me time to go the library and work on my last required research paper before dark. It's always bothered me to go to and from the campus parking lot after dark. The parking lots are so far away from the buildings and the lighting isn't that great. Shadows are everywhere. It makes me shiver to think of who, or what could be out there lurking in the shadows. I know there are security phones on several of the light poles, but they are few and far between and they still don't help that queasy feeling in the pit of my stomach.

When I get scared I like to think back to more pleasant times like the amazing Christmas I had seventeen years ago, and my fifth birthday that followed in January. My parents, my brother, and my grandparents were all together with me then. Christmas was such a wonderful day. Mom and dad had bought the *Baby Grand* piano at Christmas for me to take lessons on. That morning after the presents were opened and breakfast cleared away, mom sat down at the piano to play. She played so beautifully that it took my breath away. I wondered ... is it possible ... could I ever play like that. There was a fire burning in the fireplace. It felt so nice and warm. You could smell the pine scent from the Christmas tree, the aromas of turkey roasting in the oven, and the pies that Grandmother and mom had just baked. I can almost taste the peppermint taste of the candy canes. Oh how I long for that day again. The Christmas tree lights were blinking on and off reflecting in the mirror over the fireplace. Chris was just a baby then, about four months old. He was in a cradle near the Christmas tree and seemed completely enthralled with the blinking lights. What a sweet smile on his face. Not a care in the world.

Grandmother, Grandfather, dad and I stood around the piano while mother played and sang Christmas carols and drank warm apple cider. I remember thinking how wonderful it was to be together like that. Everything seemed so perfect. Well, I tried to sing along with them, but I only knew some of the words. I said, "I wish I could play the piano like that."Dad picked me up and gave me a great big hug and said, "You will honey, it just takes time and lots of practice, but you will play just like that a few years from now." I felt so safe and comfortable in his strong arms. I can still remember the smell of his cologne, British Sterling I believe. Everything about the house was cozy. Outside, it was snowing and you could hear the wind whistling around the corners the house. A little less than a month went by and it was my birthday, January 19th, 1992. I really didn't like having my birthday so soon after Christmas since money was usually in short supply then. The holidays almost always depleted the budget, and I can remember mom and dad talking about how it was hard for them to come up with the property taxes, the insurance and all of the other bills in January.

In spite of money problems, Mom and Dad always made life fun for me on my birthday. That year when I turned five, mom and dad had a little party for me in the afternoon. They invited three of my friends over. Heather and Judy lived just down the road about a quarter of a mile, and Meghan lived just another road further away, about another mile. There were lots of brightly colored balloons and games to play. We had sandwiches, iced cupcakes with colored sprinkles on them and ice cream. Later dad hooked Snowflake up to the wagon and we all went on a nice long hay ride. There were light snow flurries and a chill in the air. The cold chill didn't bother us though; we were all dressed warm in our snow-suits with hats, scarves, and mittens and we were wrapped up in warm blankets. Mom and Dad brought hot chocolate in thermoses for us to drink to keep us snuggly warm. Everyone was singing, laughing, and having a great time. I wish it could have lasted forever. Little did I know that tragedy soon would turn my world up-side-down?

On the way back, dad dropped my friends off at their home and then drove the horse and wagon back to the barn. Once we got home, Mom took Chris inside, gave him a bottle, dressed him in his nice warm footed pajamas, and put him to sleep in his crib upstairs. She then went back out to the barn to help dad put the wagon away, brush down Snowflake, and give him some hay. Grandmother tucked me into bed. A few minutes later I decided it would be nice to give Snowflake a treat for giving us such a great ride. I put on my slippers and robe, snuck downstairs, went into the kitchen, grabbed an apple, and ran out to the barn. The snow had just stopped. It was a dark night and kind of eerie. The sky was overcast and no moon or stars were visible in the sky. The barn door was slid open just enough for me to go in. I heard Dad talking to someone, a man. There was a lot of shouting. A lady's voice was telling mom to be quiet and then dad shouted, "No!" I heard three loud bangs. It stopped me dead in my tracks. I stood very still trying to focus my eyes in the dim light so I could see what was going on. From where I was standing though I couldn't see who was talking. I became worried and frightened. I didn't know what was going on, but I sensed it was something very bad. A small lantern was sitting on the wagon. It gave off just enough light for me to see where I was going. I wanted to head back to the house, but I was too scared to move, frozen in my step. I called out for mom and dad and just as I did, from behind me I could see a dark, black shadow; it's the one that has been haunting me for years. The next thing I knew, a man grabbed me from behind and put his hand over my mouth. I reached for his hand to pull it away, but I couldn't. He had a glove on and a cold, wet cloth in his hand over my mouth. He said, "don't scream kid, or I'll kill you."

Weeks later, I was at home and I awoke to the sweet scent of lilacs and roses from the flowers in the vase on my nightstand. Grandmother was sitting next to me on the bed. She said, "I'm so glad you are awake, you've been through so much. Do you know where you are?" I said, "Yes, I'm in my bedroom, but I feel like I've been asleep a long time." I remember wanting to fix breakfast for mom and dad. Grandmother held me close and said, "It hurts me to tell you this honey, but mommy, daddy, and Chris are gone, I'm so sorry." She was sobbing and as the tears streamed down her face she said, "That's all I can tell you." I didn't understand. I remember thinking, "Why are they gone? Where did they go? What happened?" I asked, "When are they coming back?" Grandmother said, "They are not coming back." I screamed: "What do you mean they are not coming back?" I went stumbling through the house. My legs were so weak I could hardly stand, but I kept going through the house and out to the barn before Grandmother could stop me. As I got close to the barn I could feel the hair stand up on my arms and I started to throw-up. I remembered the smell of that man's glove and cloth over my mouth and the horrible sound of his voice. The smell was strange, sweet and strong, something I will never forget. I can still hear the sound of his horrible voice echoing in my mind. It brings chills up and down my spine. That's the last thing I remember of that horrible, horrible dark night.

Chapter 4

The Perfect Reunion

Two days after graduation, a registered over-night delivery came in the mail addressed to Alice and Catherine Murphy. I asked Grandmother if I could open it. It was from Aunt Sarah and Uncle Tony in Tucson, AZ. Inside were two airplane tickets and a card attached that said: Congratulations Catherine! Now that you have been graduated from college, it's time for you and Grandmother Alice to come out to visit us. Our son just graduated from high school as well. The two of you can get to know each other. We will have a nice celebration and catch up on what's been going on with all of us. We are looking forward to seeing you both. Grandmother Alice said, "Well girl, what are you waiting for, go upstairs and start packing."

I called into work and asked for a couple of weeks of vacation. My boss, Donald Collier, said "No problem, you've been doing a great job for us. You've worked hard to get your degree and now that you have it, I hope you are ready to work for us full-time. We'll discuss your position when you return. Be safe and have a great time." That was just what I was hoping for. I was extremely excited. Finally I would get to meet some of my family.

The tickets were for a flight to leave out of Broome County Airport (Binghamton, NY) the next morning, Friday, at 7:00 am, so Grandmother and I were busy getting ready. We went shopping to get a few last minute things, and called it an early night so we could travel rested. Neither of us had flown before so the trip was going to be a new and exciting experience for both of us.

At the airport we heard, "Ladies and gentlemen we are now ready to board US Airways flight 3793 to Philadelphia." From there we would have to board flight 1543 to Phoenix. There we wouldn't have to get off the flight. Just stay on board and wait for others to disembark and more people to board, then take off again for Tucson. It would be a long day, between five to six hours of actual flight time and two hours between flights. As the plane took off from Binghamton we could see the sun rising in the East. What a spectacular view. Take-off was a little scary but once we climbed to cruising altitude it was better. The view was well worth it. After the plane reached a straight and level altitude the ground looked like a patch-work quilt and the clouds looked like massive mounds of cotton. The entire flight was marvelous, but long. As always, Grandmother was very supportive and understanding, but I think she was also a little nervous. She just said, "Don't worry honey, everything will be fine." What a sweetheart she has been to me, always. At times she has been strict with me when I needed it, but never without showing an equal amount of love and compassion.

It's Friday, a little after two pm. The flight was definitely a worthwhile experience, but exhausting. The anticipation of meeting family gave me butterflies in my stomach. When we left the disembarking area, our family was waiting for us. They were a beautiful sight. Aunt Sarah looks quite a bit like me and like mom in her pictures but with brown eyes. Uncle Tony has dark brown curly hair and is a little taller than Aunt Sarah, but not much. Chris is tall too with light blond hair and sky blue eyes.

After all of the hugs and kisses, we left for the ranch. I never imagined how different the climate and surroundings could be from that of New York. The temperature was 93 degrees, but it didn't seem as hot as it does in NY when it's 93. They attribute that feeling to it being, *a dry heat*. The ground was brown and sandy with Saguaro cactuses sticking up everywhere I looked. I'm used to green grass and green pine trees. The other difference was the mountains. They're much higher in Tucson and they looked purple. The drive to the ranch on the North West side of Tucson took close to an hour. We were getting quite hungry by this time. We only had snacks on the plane so we were looking forward to dinner. Once we got to the ranch we met the cook. Her name was Carlita, an older woman with long black hair pulled back in a beautiful long braid. Soon she brought us each a glass of ice tea and a little snack to hold us over until dinner. That was very refreshing.

The ranch house is a very Western looking two story house with a living-room, kitchen, big dining room, bathroom, and laundry room downstairs. Upstairs there are five large bedrooms and two bathrooms. Aunt Sarah showed Grandmother and me, our bedrooms. When I walked into my room I jumped on the bed right away. Oh ... how soft and comfy. The room is spacious, with an antique looking dresser on one wall, a nice size closet and wash stand on the opposite wall, a lounge chair in the corner, and my bed on the other wall. A big window was on the West wall. After we got settled in and unpacked, we went back downstairs. Carlita had fixed us a great pot roast dinner with biscuits, mashed potatoes and gravy for dinner. She said, "Tomorrow I will fix you a real southwestern dinner." We all enjoyed dinner, sat and talked for awhile and then had warm apple pie and ice cream.

Not only was the ranch house huge, the grounds were extensive. I had never seen anything like it. They have 120 acres of fenced in land, a huge barn, and a stable. Next to the barn they have all kinds of work equipment. In the stable were five beautiful riding horses and one Belgium draft work horse. Tomorrow morning we are all going for a ride. They have a ranch hand named Philip that takes care of the horses and maintains the ranch. Chris and I went for a short walk and talked. He is five years younger than me and just graduated from high school. He was very friendly and outgoing. Being with him was very comfortable. We had only just met, but it seemed like we had known each other forever. The sun was starting to set in the West. It almost looked like there were two sunsets. How strange I thought. The mountains looked purple and the sky was the most beautiful mixture of pink and orange. We never saw sunsets on the horizon like that in New York. The colors were gorgeous. We went back inside and joined the others. All of us talked and talked 'till the wee hours of the morning.

Chris and I were so excited that sleep didn't come easy. After about five hours of sleep we were up and ready to go. We decided to go horseback riding early since the temperature was expected to hit the high 90's by noon. Philip told us what we needed to know to ride them and said we could ride any horse we wanted. That was a hard choice. They have a quarter horse that was a little taller and leaner than the rest, with a large jaw and small ears, named Ghost; an Appaloosa (developed by the Nez Perce Indians of the American North West) with dark brown spots on a white coat, named Biscuit; a three-gaited thoroughbred of the American Saddle-bred breed, named Buster; an Arabian breed that is smaller than the other riding horses, but has a shorter, stronger back, named Queenie; and a Tennessee Walker named, King. After a lot of thinking: I chose Queenie, Chris decided on King, Grandmother Alice liked Biscuit, Aunt Sarah chose Ghost, and Uncle Tony took Buster. For me, this was probably the best ride of my life. All of the horses were well trained and responded to our commands with no problems. I have to admit I was a little nervous and saddle-sore by the time we were through, but it was a fantastic ride around the ranch. The trail went for what seemed like miles up and over a couple rolling hills and around the pond and back to the stables. Once we got back to the stables Philip unsaddled and brushed the horses. It was getting quite hot by this time and Chris took off his shirt to cool off. To my surprise I saw dimples in his shoulders. I said, Chris, those are just like mine. My brother, my dad and my Grandfather had them also. However, I wasn't about to show him mine. He said he thought those were just a defect he was born with. Everyone laughed.

Later that night after dinner ... Grandmother, Aunt Sarah and Uncle Tony said we needed to have a talk. We all gathered around the long table in the dining room. Carlita brought in a choice of ice tea, lemonade, or water for us. After a few minutes, Aunt Sarah said one of the reasons she wanted us to come out to Arizona was to celebrate both graduations. But, the most important reason was for Chris and me to meet, that we were brother and sister. You could have knocked me over with a feather. I couldn't believe what I just heard. Chris looked as shocked as I was. I said, why didn't someone tell us this before? Chris said, "You've got to be kidding, I didn't even know I had a sister." For so long, I had wanted to know what happened to my brother. Grandmother knew that was why Aunt Sarah had sent for us. Aunt Sarah said, "It was time." This meeting had been planned seventeen years ago, but everyone was sworn to secrecy. The story came out that when mom died and dad disappeared, Aunt Sarah and Uncle Tony adopted Chris. Aunt Sarah desperately wanted a baby and Chris was the perfect addition to her family. Grandmother Alice could handle me since I was five, but Chris was still a lot of work. He was still in diapers. Mom had just finished nursing him a few weeks before that awful night. He wasn't sleeping through the night yet, and adjusting to new parents wouldn't be that difficult for him at five months of age. Everyone decided it would be too much for Grandmother to handle the both of us. Over the years no-one had told Chris or me anything. They thought that if we knew about each other we would want to be together immediately and that wasn't possible until now. What a shock ... but how wonderful the news. Chris looked at me and I stared back at him. We were both overwhelmed. I started to cry, but they were tears of joy. This was a family reunion made in heaven.

After the initial revelation, Chris and I had a lot to discuss. No-one had told him that he was adopted, let alone anything about my mother and father. He didn't know he had a sister. He was really still in shock. He wondered why Aunt Sarah and Uncle Tony hadn't told him before now. I had trouble believing that this was real, myself. I was greatly offended that Grandmother Alice had not told me that Chris was adopted by Aunt Sarah and Uncle Tony. That he was alive and living out here in Arizona. I felt a little betrayed that she didn't think I should have been told. "Why didn't she tell me?" After talking for quite awhile Chris and I decided that since we had no say in the matter, we just needed to accept what we couldn't change and move on, but Chris would talk later to his mom about it, and I would talk more with Grandmother Alice about it. We needed to focus on something else. We would embark on a new adventure, to find out what happened to our parents.

Chris and I vowed that tomorrow would be a new beginning for both of us. We would make up for years we didn't know we were brother and sister. We would spend as much time as possible with each other from now on and begin our search.

Chapter 5

The Search Is On

In the morning we sat down with Aunt Sarah and Uncle Tony and ask them to help us find out what happened to our parents. Uncle Tony thought a good place to start would be to call his brother, Todd Taylor, who was a detective for the Phoenix Police Department. He called Todd and explained a little of the murder, missing person, kidnapping case to him and asked for his help. Uncle Tony asked Uncle Todd if he would be willing to come to Tucson and meet with the family. He said "Yes, if I can clear my schedule." He called back an hour later and said he would be down to meet with us the first thing in the morning.

I knew Chris was going through something entirely different from me so I tried to back off a little, but it was hard. I had so many questions to ask him. Just learning that he was adopted was enough to overwhelm anyone let alone finding out about me. I tried to help him understand what I already knew, that my grandparents would never have given him to Aunt Sarah if it wasn't necessary. I remember him as a baby and I knew they loved him. They must have had no choice. It was all a horrible nightmare. Aunt Sarah and Uncle Tony have been wonderful to Chris and it was obvious that he loves them very much. As far as he's concerned they are still his parents, but he now knows he had biological parents also. We both knew that our family would never do anything intentionally to hurt us, so after talking to Aunt Sarah and Grandmother Alice, we realized that everyone only wanted what was best for us. They must have made the best decisions possible for everyone under the circumstances. It was 11:00 pm and we were both pretty exhausted. We decided it was the time for bed.

I hadn't slept much, tossing and turning all night. When I awoke at dawn still spinning from yesterday's news, I got up, threw on some clothes and slipped out of the house. Chris was already up and outside. "This is the day ..." I thought, "Oh my heavens this is actually the first day of our search for news of our parents. Uncle Todd is coming here. Hopefully he will be able to help us." It was pretty obvious that we both were at a loss to know exactly what we needed to say or ask Uncle Todd. I felt like I needed time to think things through, but really I just knew that I wanted what I had wanted for the last seventeen years. I wanted to know what happened that night. Chris wanted to know the same things I did. Staring into thin air for a moment, the shrill cry of a hawk high overhead pulled me into awareness. Chris said, "Are you alright?" I said, "I think so. Are you?" He said, "I guess so, but I'm still feeling shocked and a little scared. I started to hyper-ventilate, just trying to process everything." We gave each other a great big hug, one that I don't think either one of us wanted to let go of. We seemed to have such a strong bond for only knowing each other for such a short while, but it all seemed so right. We both had tears in our eyes when we looked at each other. "What shall we do know, Chris asked?" I think our next step is just to wait until we can talk to Todd this morning and hear what he has to say.

It had rained last night. The air was fresh with the smell of mesquite. The sky was clear and a beautiful blue. The tree next to the stable was a stunning bright green. Philip later told me it was a Palo Verde tree. Even the trunk and bark were green. That is so unlike the trees in NY. My slippers got wet as I splashed through the puddles crossing the dirt driveway to the corral. I quickly climbed up to the top round of the fence and sat down. Chris was right behind me. I heard something, a voice. "Who's there?" I said. "Hello! Just me", said Philip. "I didn't mean to frighten you Catherine. I was just talking to Queenie, she's such a sweet horse, you know." Just then, Queenie walked through the stable door into the corral and over to me, nudging my knee with her nose. I petted her for awhile and the tension and nervousness I had been feeling seemed to pass ... at least for now. Chris was petting her too. Philip said, "She likes you, you know." I said, "Yes, I think so. I really enjoyed riding her yesterday. Well ... I guess it's time for us to go back in and get cleaned up for breakfast. What do you think Chris?" "Yes I guess so," he said.

I found the hot shower very nice and refreshing. It felt different. I think the warm water system had a water softener in it. As the water flowed over my skin, it was a very smooth feeling, and the water pressure was great. I dressed and headed to the kitchen. Just as I came through the door, Chris met me at the top of the stairs. Chris said, "I'm having a little trouble wrapping my head around all this. I may have been adopted, but Aunt Sarah and Uncle Tony have been great parents. I've been nobody's dream-child. About a year ago, I saw a diary mother was keeping, at least I thought she was my mother. She's the only mother I've ever known. In the diary, she mentioned how so many of the things I did worried her. I grew up very stubborn and completely unpredictable. I think I was more than she bargained for. I know we don't have time right now, but I have so many stories to tell you, and there's so much I want to hear from you. For now though, we had better go downstairs for breakfast. The first time we have a chance, we need to have another talk." Catherine said, "Ok, right after breakfast."

By the time we got to the kitchen, everyone was already seated at the table. Aunt Sarah said, "Come on in and please be seated." Uncle Tony led us in prayer giving thanks for breakfast and thanks that we were all finally together. "Wow, what a spread I thought." There were pancakes, fresh strawberries and whip cream for the pancakes if we wanted them, eggs, toast, bacon, chorizo, and a fruit-and-cinnamon quesadilla. I tried a little of everything, but couldn't eat too much. I was just way too excited. Just as we finished breakfast, Todd pulled up out front.

Todd gathered us all together in the living room. He called it the *great room*. Understandably so ... it is huge, about 36 feet square with a big fireplace on one end. Todd said, "Tony explained a little of what was going on, but I still have a lot of questions to ask all of you. Hope you don't mind, but I will be taping our conversations, that way I won't forget any important details." Grandmother Alice was the first to speak. She talked about how my dad had completed his training in the Marines at Paris Island, South Carolina, and then went to Camp Pendleton in California. She said, "I believe it's somewhere north of the Marine Corp Recruitment Depot (MCRD)." She then related the following: "Ted's first deployment was to Bosnia. After completing his first tour of duty he came back and was home for three weeks before being deployed to Bosnia for another tour. The first and second tour added up to eight years. Coming back from Bosnia he was different, more mature, more reserved. The next day he proposed to his lifelong sweetheart, my lovely daughter-in-law, Joyce. They were wed six months later. Within days he had applied for several different jobs and was hired by IBM, commonly known as, 'Big Blue' in Endicott. The job seemed very challenging and very fulfilling for him. Joyce was teaching at the local university and everything was great. One year later, Catherine was born. We were all so very happy. About a year after that, a friend from the Marines came for a visit. His name was Matt something. I can't remember his last name. He stayed for about a week and then he and Ted took off for a few days and went fishing, where they could reminisce about old times, I guess. We didn't see Matt again after that. Ted was promoted to sales at IBM and soon was gone for about two weeks out of every month. The money was good and Ted told Joyce they needed to start putting money away for retirement and Catherine's education. They lived with us on the farm where he grew up to save money. That worked out well for them and for us too, that way the extra income would help us with the maintenance and upkeep on the house and property etc., so it wasn't so hard on Grandfather Edwin and me. I'm sure that we were an additional burden on Ted and Joyce financially, and they didn't have the privacy they probably wanted at times, but they said they loved all of us living together and everything would be fine. Still, after a few years Ted seemed to be bothered by something and we didn't know what. Over the next year or so it got worse. On August 19th, 1991, Joyce gave birth to Chris. Ted's spirits perked up for awhile. We had a wonderful Christmas that year but then on Catherine's birthday in January everything came to a screeching halt."

Todd took Grandmother Alice aside to have her relate that tragic incident in the barn to him in private. One by one, he took each of us into the kitchen to talk to us. We each told him all we knew. When he was finished, he said, "It will take me some time to sift through all of the data I've collected and to investigate what I can from my office in Phoenix. What I can't do there, I will get in touch with some other agencies and ask for their help. Rest assured I will do everything in my power to help solve this case. You can expect to hear from me soon, probably within a few weeks after your return to New York."

Catherine said, "What a relief to know that something was actually happening. Soon I thought, soon we will know something."

Catherine said to Chris, "Let's talk some more; ...now is a good time." Chris said, "I've got to say ... last night really spooked me, but it brought things into perspective for me. Please listen, but don't judge me, ok? I was thinking about something that I used to do when I was little boy. It kind of goes against the way mom has raised me, because I don't think she believes superstition. ... About a year ago, her diary was left open on the end table, so I read what was on the open page. It said, 'I think if we inspire Chris with enough religious doctrine, he won't be perverted by superstition.' I don't know that I'm superstitious, but I've felt for years that a part of me was missing and now I know that what I was missing was family. Please don't think I'm crazy, ok? Before I was old enough to go to school I would sit alone on my bed at night and as the sun was going down ... the sunrays slanting across the fields and through my bedroom window ... I would sing a tune, a very simple tune that I made up, to my imaginary brother named Ted."

"Chris" Catherine said, "Our father's name is Ted. Oh, my gosh! I've got goose bumps all over me. I definitely don't think you are crazy for feeling like something was missing and having an imaginary brother just filled the emptiness you felt. I have felt this same kind of emptiness for the last seventeen years. Someday, I'll tell you some of my crazy stories." We both laughed.

Chapter 6

Chain of Command for
Inquiring Minds

Todd Taylor is a detective, but not a typical gumshoe. He's highly qualified, experienced, and is full of passionate energy. He has a reputation for being the most thorough and methodical of detectives. His professionalism and expert methods of solving crimes is legendary, one that many other detectives can only envy. He's worked with the Phoenix Police Department for twenty years, five as a beat cop and fifteen as a detective, and has solved many career making and complex cases.

When Todd arrived at his office he reviewed the tapes and organized all of the information he had collected at his brother's ranch in Tucson. His next step was to review any pertinent reports that he could collect from other police agencies. He searched police records from 19 Jan, 1992 in Vestal, NY. The records were from the Sheriff Department's original investigation. The initial report alleged murder and kidnapping along with numerous supplemental police reports including forensic reports, an autopsy report, a medical report, a CPS report, a veterinary report and a summary report. The reports stated that Joyce Murphy had been killed, Catherine Murphy kidnapped and Snowball (their horse) killed. No demands were made. The autopsy showed the cause of death for Joyce to be gunshot wounds to the head and torso. Catherine had been taken by unknown kidnapper(s). The supplemental police and CPS reports showed that at 3:00 am the following day, she was left anonymously at the emergency room of Binghamton General Hospital. She was found to be in a state of catatonic withdrawal. The Medical reports said there were no indications of sexual molestation, but that there were bruises around her face and arms. Ted was listed as a missing person and not eliminated from involvement in the incident. The Veterinary report stated that Snowflake died of suffocation from an injection of butorphanol. At initial response, the basic report said the bullets, empty cartridges and other evidence from the scene had been sent to the lab for analysis. The motive(s) for the murder and kidnapping were unknown or at least not mentioned. The latest report showed the active status of the investigation had been terminated upon exhaustion of all leads.

After reviewing all of the information, Todd decided to contact Sheriff Montgomery, at the Broome County Sheriff Office (S. O.). Todd believed that since the murder took place in Broome County, Sheriff Montgomery had primary jurisdiction in the case. It remains inactive as a cold case. Todd explained to Sheriff Montgomery, his family ties with the Murphy's and his interest in reactivating the case.

Todd now decided that the best move would be to contact his friend Clyde Duncan at the FBI in Phoenix. Todd shared the information he had found with Clyde, who was the Special Agent in Charge (SAIC). Clyde found the case interesting and said he would investigate the case through his office. Clyde obtained Ted Murphy's finger prints from FBI files and discovered that they matched those of someone else in the NCIC Database, Steve Mason. He had been involved in a bar fight back in 1991 and was arrested and fingerprinted. Steve Mason's fingerprint records revealed that he and Ted Murphy were one in the same.

Indexes showed Murphy was also connected to some other federal records. With this new information, SAIC Clyde Duncan felt the investigation should be reactivated and called S. A. James (Jim) Walker, his former partner and a convenient contact in the Albany FBI office. Jim was glad to have heard from his old partner and friend and opened an FBI file.

S. A. James Walker placed a call to S. A. Carrie Wagner at the FBI Office in Binghamton bringing her up-to-speed. He then called Broome County Sheriff Montgomery, the original investigator at the crime scene back in January, 1992. After discussing the case with him for a little while, Sheriff Montgomery said, "I think it would be advisable to start a *task force*, but I really don't have the resources here to do any more than I did back in 1992. With your immediate access to the federal records necessary to accomplish the task, I would like you to assist in starting the task force. I'll pass the investigation to you, if you are willing." James Walker said he would get back in touch with Sheriff Montgomery after he talked with SAIC Clyde Duncan.

James Walker knew two Special Agents in Albany perfect for the job, S. A. Trent McGuire and S. A. Kassidy Barnes who specialize in cold case investigations. Clyde Duncan gave James Walker permission to assign the two Special Agents in Albany to head the task force.

Trent McGuire and Kassidy Barnes first met when they were assigned to work together five years ago and have solved numerous cold case crimes together, some of which required them to be brave and to use ingenuity in their methods. Their actions gained the confidence of their superiors which allowed them a great deal of latitude for solving future cases.

Trent McGuire is 5' 11" and weighs about 175 lbs. He has auburn hair, freckles, and green eyes. He always wears polo shirts with kakis, *Nike* sneakers; and at this time of year (spring) his favorite *Forty-Niners* jacket. Kassidy Barnes is 5' 7" and weighs about 130 lbs. She has black hair, dimples in her cheeks, purple/blue eyes; wears tight *Gloria Vanderbilt* jeans, a turtleneck sweater, a light weight jacket and *Sketchers* shoes. In their special job assignment they are both exempt from the traditional FBI dress code. They both work out regularly to keep in shape and fit enough to run at a seconds notice. Though they have a great deal in common, their dissimilar traits, such as personal interests and background, allow them to offer varying perspectives to their cases. Their total personalities plus their composite philosophy of investigation makes them great partners.

As part of a task force it's important for our two Special Agent's, Trent McGuire and Kassidy Barnes to keep the communication flowing with all of the others involved. Those would include: Detective Todd in Phoenix, SAIC Clyde Duncan, S. A. James Walker, S. A. Carrie Wagner and Sheriff Montgomery. This would be no problem for our Special Agents.

Trent and Kassidy spent several days reviewing all of the records compiled so far. Kassidy said, "We need more information." However, further records on Steve Mason required a clearance level that is usually assigned to CIA supervisors only, an indication to us that Steve Mason was more than likely, a CIA Operative. This would require an unusual level of interagency cooperation or a Federal Court Order to take a closer look. The latter could take a long time to acquire. They were convinced that this case was quite a bit more complicated than their usual cases and would probably be a little more challenging. For them though, that only meant more interest and excitement.

The first step for our team was to investigate the bar fight and domestic violence case from 1991. The local police record showed that it took place in Donnelly's Shamrock Pub, in Peoria, Illinois. The fight started out as an argument and then got physical between Steve Mason, and Marine Major Matt McGuire.

Major Nicki James, was there but not involved in the altercation. Police records showed Steve Mason (Ted Murphy) and Marine Matt McGuire had been friends for years and served together in Bosnia, and Syria. Trent and Kassidy said they would try and track down Major Matt McGuire and Major Nicki James and see if they could get any more information on Ted (Steve Mason).

While Trent and Kassidy took off for Peoria, James Walker decided to meet again with Carrie Wagner. They discussed their records together and scheduled a visit with Sheriff Montgomery. They let the sheriff know they were going to interview Alice Murphy and Catherine and do another search of the premises.

Chapter 7

Returning Home

Catherine and Alice arrive back in Binghamton after their exciting and rewarding trip to Arizona. They reminisce about all of their sightseeing adventures including: The Desert Museum, Old Tucson, Biosphere 2, Kartchner Caverns, Out of Africa Wildlife Park, the Grand Canyon, Tombstone, and The Air & Space Museum. Most importantly, they delight in having been reacquainted with family. Catherine and Alice have brought back loads of memorabilia to make a scrap book and share a fantastic video of most of the trip. It's comforting to look at all of these, but it's even more comforting to know that Chris will be coming out to Vestal Center to visit them for the Christmas holidays.

Soon they settle in to their normal routines. Catherine meets with her boss at the Press, Donald Collier. After discussing her trip, Donald informs her that he has an open editor's position for a new section of the paper, *Citizen's Voices*. "Having apprenticed for three years in a similar position I am offering you the job, probationary for three months with a salary commensurate with other beginning editors here at the paper. If we like your work and you like the job we will make the promotion permanent and you will be given a $10.00/hour raise. Would you like the position, Catherine?" "Oh wow, I wasn't expecting that. But yes,

yes! Thank you!" "I would like you to start, Monday, how's that sound to you?" "That sounds wonderful, sir." Donald Collier said, "Great Catherine, see you Monday."

Later that afternoon Catherine heads home. She's on *Cloud Nine*. It seems as though her life couldn't get any better. As soon as she entered the door, Catherine shared her good news with Grandmother Alice. "How wonderful," Grandmother Alice said, "When are you going to take me to Hawaii?" Upon my pause, ... Grandmother said, "Only joking" and chuckled. As usual, when Catherine arrived home, dinner was waiting for her. After dinner while they were relaxing, there was a knock on the door.

When Catherine answered the door, a man and a woman where standing there. As they showed Catherine their badges, they introduced themselves: "I'm Special Agent James Walker with the FBI in Albany and this is Special Agent Carrie Wagner with the FBI in Broome County. May we come in?" Catherine said, "First, tell me why you are here?" James Walker said, "We have been assigned to a special task force headed by special agents, Trent McGuire and Kassidy Barnes. The case has been reactivated for us to further investigate what happened in January, 1992. I was advised that Detective Todd in Phoenix had informed you." "Yes, we heard from Detective Todd yesterday. We're just surprised to see you so soon. We will be glad to help you in any way we can. Please come in. I am Catherine." As Grandmother Alice entered the room, Catherine introduced her to the Special Agents.

Grandmother Alice asked the agents to make themselves comfortable and offered them some ice tea. James Walker said, "We would like to ask you some questions, if we may. We have already spoken with Sheriff Montgomery and we reviewed the reports in the case, but we still have some questions. Alice ... please tell us what you can about your son and his wife?"

"Well, Ted and Joyce were high-school sweethearts. After graduation, they both went on to college at the local State University and dated on and off for about four years. Ted achieved his BA in Liberal Arts with a minor in languages, and went on to get a Master's in Languages. He had attended the Marine's ROTC Program, so he went directly into the Marine's after graduation. Joyce completed her BA in Education and a Master's in Behavioral Sciences. After graduation she started teaching at the University. They were very much in love the whole time, almost inseparable, but neither was ready to get married. Ted was fluid in five languages and that led him to his assignments in Bosnia and Syria as a linguist for the Marines. He would come home from time-to-time on leave. He and Joyce would see a lot of each other then and it would kind of rekindle their relationship. They both seemed to grow up over those years and their relationship matured. After Ted's second tour, when he returned from Bosnia, he decided not to re-enlist. He said, he was finished with the military. That was when he proposed to Joyce. They were so happy. They were married on Valentine's Day, 1987. They moved in with us right after the honeymoon. They couldn't have been a sweeter couple. They doted over each other, so lovingly, doing everything possible to please each other. It seemed like a marriage made in heaven. Joyce found out she was pregnant in May of that year and Catherine was born January 19th, 1988. The relationship seemed to blossom even more."

"It was the perfect little family. I don't know what more I can tell you about their relationship. The last couple of years, things were a little strained, with his job taking him out of town so much. They talked on the phone a lot though. There were times when we wouldn't hear from him for two or three weeks, but I think he was just busy with work. I know for a short time he had some financial investment decisions to make, but I'm sure those were resolved. He was putting quite a bit of money away for retirement and the children's education. It was always a happy reunion when he came home, but the last five or six months he seemed troubled ... depressed even. He would come in, give Joyce a quick peck on the cheek, rush upstairs, make a phone call and a short time later come down, fix himself a stiff drink and play his violin to relax. What followed was his favorite pastime, playing with Catherine. She was the apple-of-his-eye. They would play for awhile and Ted would take her up to bed, read a bedtime story to her, listen to her prayer and come back downstairs to spend time with Joyce. He said that when he was in a bad mood or depressed, it had nothing to do with us, that it was just something to do with his work. I already told all of this to Todd in Phoenix." SAIC Clyde Duncan said, "Yes, we know Alice, we read your interview, but we wanted to hear it from you and find out if you remembered any more details about their relationship or about the kidnapping?"

Grandmother Alice said, "Let's go in the kitchen to talk about this over a cup of tea. I will never forget the events of Catherine's kidnapping. They are burned into my memory forever. Grandfather Edwin and I were talking in the kitchen; I had just tucked Catherine into bed a few minutes before that. We heard shots coming from the barn. We rushed outside just in time to see a black SUV speeding away from behind the barn and out beyond the driveway to the road in front of the house. Catherine's favorite Cabbage Patch doll, She called it, 'Sherri', was caught in the back door. We could see it as the van pulled away. I knew the doll was hers because Joyce and I had just made a new outfit for it; a red coat snow suit with white fur around the collar, cuffs, and the bottom of the jacket. Ted came storming past us screaming that Joyce had been shot and Catherine kidnapped. My first thought was that's impossible, that can't be Catherine's doll, she's upstairs asleep. I ran into the house and upstairs to make sure Catherine was sound asleep, but she wasn't there. She wasn't there! At first Ed and I were in shock, but we called the sheriff. Ed and I ran back outside towards the barn.

Just then Ted ran up to us kissed us, said goodbye and drove off. We thought he went after the kidnappers. We haven't seen him since. Ed and I ran out to the barn, the door was open, and we walked in far enough to see ... there was just enough light to see the bloody shape of Joyce lying on the ground by the wagon. Just then the sheriff pulled up in the driveway. We ran out to meet him. I was hysterical and screamed, 'Joyce is lying on the barn floor all bloody, ...she may be dead, Catherine is missing and Ted is gone!' By this time, more sheriff's deputies and special investigators were here. They searched the house and barn. They wouldn't let Ed and me anywhere near the crime scene, but we knew ... somehow, someone had kidnapped Catherine ... she must have been in that van. God only, knows why someone would want to take her, such a little girl, our little angel. The police called for a K9 search dog. A policeman soon arrived with the search dog. After all of the evidence was collected from the barn, I gave the police some of Catherine's clothing for the dog to get her scent. The dog led the officers to the area behind the barn where the black SUV must have been parked. The kidnappers must have carried Catherine, because there were only two men's boot prints, and a woman's high heal prints leading to and from the barn to the van. Police followed the tracks in the snow. They led to where we saw the vehicle speeding away, out to the road. The investigators took lots of pictures and even made casts of the vehicle tracks and foot prints. Ed and I were numb. It was days before we would take it all in."

"About 4:00 am the following morning, Sheriff Montgomery got a call from Binghamton General Hospital. A little girl, about five years old had been brought in anonymously and left on the floor in the emergency room. A man just brought her in and took off. He had a mask on, so no one got a good look at him, but they had a description of his approximate height, weight and clothes. The attendant ran outside, but only saw a black SUV driving away."

"Sheriff Montgomery called about 6:00 am and asked if we would like to go to the hospital with him to see if the little girl was Catherine. Of course we said, "Yes." We were still reeling from the events of the night before, but raced to the hospital. The sheriff was already there and was questioning the hospital staff. The doctor led us to the intensive care unit. When I saw the little girl, I burst into tears. It was Catherine. Ed put his arms around me and we both just sobbed and sobbed. She was hooked up to all kinds of life support equipment. Doctor Chadwick said she was in a catatonic withdrawal state. I had no idea what that meant. He also said that she had not been sexually molested. I must have fainted, because the next thing I remembered was a nurse passing smelling salts under my nose. This was the most terrible night of my life. I just knew I couldn't take any more bad news. Ed and I went in to see Catherine. Her little arms and face were so bruised, she had a black eye and there was a cut on her lip. Then even worse news came, the doctors had no idea when or if she would ever come out of the catatonic state. Her eyes were open, but staring straight ahead. They didn't move. She looked scared-to-death." Sheriff Montgomery said, "The police describe it as *three-whites,* or *like-a-deer-in-headlights.*" Dr. Chadwick said, "Fear is probably what caused her condition. Catatonia, or catatonic withdrawal is often the result of a traumatic and terrifying experience. Severe fear causes the psyche to withdraw, to protect the patient from what is happening to them. She's in kind of a cataleptic stupor where the musculature becomes hypotonic. They can tell more from an FMRI. This will tell us the extent of her condition." Grandmother Alice said, "We were told we would just have to be patient and wait for any improvement in her condition. It could be days or even weeks."

"For weeks we prayed, and watched, and waited by her bedside. It was days before we could eat and keep anything down. We were both sick and had trouble sleeping. We tried to sleep, but every time we closed our eyes, we would see Joyce laying there in the barn, shot to death, all bloody and Catherine laying in that hospital bed with tubes coming to and from her to the machines. Just to see the bruises and thinking about what she must have gone through gave us nightmares and caused our chest to tighten. The doctors gave us something to help us sleep, but it was still hard to get past the memories of that *blackest of nights*."

"After two weeks, Catherine awoke from the catatonic state, but still was not very coherent. When the doctors asked her questions, she would just shake her head yes or no and cried, "Mommy." She wouldn't speak otherwise. With the medications and side-stepping her requests for "Mommy", we were able to avoid telling her about her mother's death. Her facial expression exhibited fear and gloom and her eyes were dark and sunken. After a couple of days she started to respond verbally. It would take some time for her to recover. To this day she has been unable to relate to us exactly what happened. It must still be too painful for her to remember. At the end of the third week we were able to take her home, but she still needed more physical therapy to strengthen her legs. For several weeks after she was released from the hospital, a psychiatrist, Dr. Evelyn Moyer, worked with her."

The morning after we brought her home I wanted everything to be perfect for her. I had her favorite flowers, lilacs and roses, in a vase on the night stand by her bed, and all of her favorite stuffed animals were lined up next to her so she could see them. I was sitting next to her on the bed, holding her hand when she woke up. She had a look on her face that I hadn't seen before. It was as though she awoke in a strange place and had no idea what she was doing there. It was then that I realized that she had no memory of her hospital stay or the kidnapping. Tears swelled in my eyes. I ask her, "Honey, do you know where you are?"She paused for a minute and said, "Hi Grandmother Alice …yes, I'm in my bedroom, but I feel like I've been sleeping a long time. Is it time for breakfast? My party was so nice yesterday, let's go downstairs and make breakfast for mommy and daddy and surprise them." I knew then, that I needed to tell her about her parents, but I thought: how do you tell a little five year old girl that her mother is dead, her father is missing, and her brother is gone? I knew she would be looking for them as soon as she got out of bed, so I had no choice; I had to tell her right then. I held her snuggly in my arms and told her softly that they were gone. I knew she wanted to know more, but she was in such a fragile state I couldn't tell her anymore."

Agent Walker and Agent Wagner thanked Alice for talking to them. Walker asked to speak to Catherine. They went off into the library where they could be alone. Catherine gave her statement just as she had before in Tucson, nothing more.

Walker asked Alice if it was ok for them to make a search of the house, barn and property. They had a Federal search warrant just in case the family was not cooperative, but Alice said of course it was ok. She was more than willing to do anything that might help with the investigation. Alice left them alone to do their investigation. They wondered what the connection was between the kidnapping and the killings. Why did the kidnapper(s) kill Joyce, or did they? Was Ted in-hiding or dead? Did the same people kill Ted later on? They hoped to find a clue, any clue.

Chapter 8

Detective's Adventure

Kassidy Barnes and Trent McGuire arrived in Peoria, Illinois. It was late morning and the air had become hot and clammy. They checked into the Embassy Suites Hotel and reviewed their case files, and transcriptions of the interviews their friend S. A. James Walker had given them, plus the interview tapes and files that the Sheriff Montgomery compiled during the original investigation back in 1992.

Our audacious special agents tell their story: It's 6:00 p.m. and Donnelly's is doing a booming business. As we walked into the pub, an antique sign said, Donnelly's Drinks, Friends and Blarney; Mutton & Soda Bread 3 cents, Lodgings 4 cents, (Watch for the "Wee" People). Though the entryway was painted black, the place was very warm and hospitable. It seemed to be a pretty popular place. As we walked past pinball machines, we saw many patrons at tables and some sitting at the bar. The bar was on the right and a lot of tables for eating were on the left. There was a frame of Irish shields hanging on the wall. As we approached the bar, the bartender ask, "What will ye have mates?" We introduced ourselves, and asked him what his name was? He said, "My name is Stephen Yerly, I'm the manager for the time being." We ask him how long he had worked for Donnelly's and though a young man of about forty, he said he had worked there for the last twenty years. We showed him the pictures of Ted, Matt McGuire, and Nicki James, and asked if he had ever seen any of them? He said, "In my line of work you realize we don't talk about what we see or hear." He looked us over once or twice and we showed him our badges. We talked for a little while longer and he asked: "Why do you want to know?" We told him that Ted was missing. He said that he knew him as Steve and that he had been in *time and again* about fifteen to twenty years ago. He said that Steve had met several times with the other man in the pictures. They had gotten into a fight and were arrested one night. That same night a woman was with them. He said the one man and the woman were both in Marine uniforms, but not Steve. He remembered Steve because he used to see him a couple of times a month and most of the time, he would meet with a different man in a long trench coat and hat. Stephen said they would always sit at the same table over there (Stephen pointing) in the corner, have a few drinks, talk for about a half hour, the guy in the trench coat would leave and Steve would stay and have dinner and then leave. The guy in the trench coat always carried a briefcase and would give Steve some papers or something. They never caused any trouble. Stephen said, "Steve was always very pleasant. I actually got to like the guy and he always left pretty good tips. All of the waitresses liked him too. He was the perfect gentleman. Once in awhile he would just come in for a drink or two and then leave. About four or five weeks would go by and the guy in uniform would come in to meet with Steve. They would only talk for a half hour or so and then leave. Then that one night when the guy Marine came in with the lady Marine everything was different. Steve seemed upset to see them here. An argument started. I thought maybe it was over the woman, but then voices were raised and I overheard Steve say something to do with Bosnia and the war. He said he never wanted to be a part of it and wanted out. The fists started flying. I tried to break it up, but man ... Steve was one strong dude. I ended up with a split lip and a black eye. I had Angie, my head waitress call the cops. She no longer works here; she died a few years back."

Trent asks Stephen, "Did you see any of them in here after that?" Stephen said, "About a month later Steve came back in and apologized to me and the owner for the fight and offered to pay for the damages, but we told him it was covered under our insurance. He was in just once more after that with the lady Marine. It was sometime after New Year's, about 1992. She came in and he greeted her. He seemed pretty upset and they left together." We asked Stephen why he felt Steve was upset. Stephen replied, "Because … Steve shouted, 'they've got her!' I pay close attention to Steve when he comes in after what happened before. I didn't want anything to get out of hand again. They both jumped up, she grabbed his arm and they left. I've seen her here several times since. A few of those times, she was with the other Marine. I think she must live somewhere nearby because I've seen her here and in town, out of uniform, a few times. I also saw her once riding a bicycle." Trent said, "What makes you so sure it was her. Stephen replied, "With that red hair and green eyes … with her looks and figure, she does stand out in a crowd if you know what I mean." Trent: "You wouldn't happen to know her name or where she lives would you?" Stephen: "No, but I think it might be on the police report from that night." Trent: "Thanks a lot you've been a great help." Stephen: "Hope you find the guy. He really is a nice guy."

Kassidy said, "Let's go back to the hotel and in the morning we'll check out the Peoria PD and the area around Donnelly's Pub."

The next morning we checked in with local PD in the morning. Their case report mentioned that Major Nicki James was a US Marine Intelligence Analyst, and that Steve Mason was listed as a CIA Operative. They didn't have any other useful information listed for us on Major Matt McGuire.

The address on the police report given for Nicki James was 6850 W. University St. in Peoria Heights. As we approached the address we saw the mailman delivering the mail. We waited across the street until he left and then checked the mailbox. The name on the mail was N. James. We knocked on the door… no one answered. We decided to stake out the place from across the street and wait. We've worked stakeouts together many times before so this was nothing new for us. Fortunately neither of us smoke and we like the same type of food and music, so being together for long periods of time works for us. On long stakeouts like this one, when one of us sleeps the other stays awake.

About 1:30 am, Kassidy wakes Trent. She sees a car slow and it pulls into the driveway at the house across the street. The woman isn't in uniform, and her hair is long and curled unlike the photo they had, but with the light on the post by the driveway, the color of her hair looks right. They both get out of the car and approach her as she goes to the door of the house.

"Nicki, Major Nicki James!" Trent said, "Can we have a few minutes of your time? We would just like to ask you a few questions." We showed our badges and introduced ourselves. After a few minutes she said, "Let's go inside, we may draw too much attention out here." She invited us in, and said, "I don't know where you're getting your information; I'm Lieutenant Colonel Niki James, How can I help you?" Trent said, "I'm S. A. Trent McGuire and this is S. A. Kassidy Barnes with the FBI. We showed her pictures of Steve Mason and Major Matt McGuire and asked her what she could tell us about them." Lt Col James paused. Trent said, "Don't try to deny it. We have witnesses placing you with Steve Mason and Major McGuire. Kassidy asked Lt Col James, "Now that you are a Lieutenant Colonel, are you still a US Marine Intelligence Analyst?" She said, "Yes I am." Trent said, "We know that you worked closely with Steve Mason (aka Ted Murphy), a linguist for the Marines and with Major McGuire. You can talk to us here or you go down to the station and talk to us there. We know you, Steve Mason, and Major McGuire were all in the Marine's back in 1984 together. Would you care to start there?" Lt Col James said, "There is so much more to it than that and there is no way that I can discuss it with you. It's classified and top secret." Trent told her what happened to Joyce and Catherine and ask her how that was tied in with her and the Marines. Lt Col James said, "Mason told me what happened to Joyce and Catherine. ... God knows I am so saddened about that. All I can tell you is that Steve Mason was Marine Captain Ted Murphy when I first worked with him. He became Steve Mason when he joined Force Recon Co. and when I last saw him he was working as an operative with the CIA. Yes, we were all together at Donnelly's Pub, and yes I did meet with Operative Mason in January of 1992, but I can't discuss it with you. I'm very sorry, but you're going to have to talk to someone higher up the chain-of-command than me. You need to talk to Colonel David F. Marshall of the Marine's Force Recon Co. in Virginia. Tell him what you told me and that I sent you." She gave Trent a card with Colonel Marshall's information on it. Trent then asked, "Can you at least tell us if Operative Mason is dead or alive?" Lt Col James repeated her generic response, "I can't discuss that with you, you'll have to ask Colonel Marshall."

Our next step is to contact Marine Colonel David F. Marshall in Virginia. Hopefully he will be able to help us. We went back to the hotel feeling a little confused, but a lot closer to our goal. Maybe, just maybe ... Colonel Marshall will be able to give us a lot more information and hopefully it will be good news?

Chapter 9

Colonel David F. Marshall
Candidly Speaks

Lt Col Nicki James seems to have told Kassidy and Trent as much as she could, or at least all that she was allowed to, but it wasn't enough. We had to get in to see Colonel Marshall at Quantico, Virginia, a base located in the Virginia woods along the Potomac River. It's a major base for Marine Corps training and leadership.

Morning came early for Kassidy and Trent. It's now 5:30 am and they are off to get coffee and a head-start on the day. Knowledge and instinct are what it's all about for these Special Agents. Trent said, "My gut tells me we have three options. Ted is either being held hostage by some group, he's in prison, or he's dead." Emphatically, Kassidy said, "You know what? Maybe there's another option. What if he just ran away after Joyce was killed and doesn't want to be found? Or … maybe he just got involved with the wrong people, possibly some rebellious group, while he was looking for revenge and he decided to stay with them. What ever happened, I'm confident, we will find answers. What do you think Trent?" "You're exactly right Kas, we will find answers."

Kassidy and Trent contacted James Walker, Detective Todd, and Clyde Duncan to let them know that they had found Nicki James and what was going on. Next they were on their way to Virginia. Kassidy said, "So, the plan is to meet with Colonel Marshall first. If he won't or can't tell us any more information about Ted, we can check in with our friend, S. A. Harris of the Naval Criminal Investigative Service (NCIS). His office is right there at Quantico.

The Marine Base and a NCIS Contingency Response Field Office (CRFO) are both located at Quantico, VA. Special Agent Harris has an office at the CRFO. His team provides deployable investigative support in high-risk environments around the globe, and his special agents received specialized training to prepare them for service in overseas combat and contingency environments. They are federal law enforcement professionals who report directly to the Secretary of the Navy. They have primary investigative and counterintelligence responsibilities within the Department of the Navy and frequently work with other federal, state and local law enforcement agencies.[2]

Colonel Marshall or S. A. Harris, or both, with all of their resources can and hopefully will, give us some insight into the disappearance of Ted.

Kassidy and Trent arrived at Quantico, VA by 8:30 am and were met by Corporal Lindsay Weaver. She escorted them to Colonel Dave Marshall's office. Colonel Marshall was gracious enough to listen to the story as Kassidy and Trent told it. When they were finished, Colonel Marshall went to the file cabinet, pulled out the drawer and removed a red folder. He placed the folder on the desk in front of them and said, "This is a very complicated case. I know you have been asking a lot of questions and making a lot of waves. Before we go further, I need you to understand that everything you are about to hear and read concerns National Security and is top secret. It must remain that way. So, what you hear and see in here today stays in here. Do you agree and can I count on your silence? (A few seconds pass) If not, then you need to leave right now! Kassidy and Trent both said, "We understand perfectly, thank you sir!"

Colonel Marshall got up out of his chair and walked to the window. He stared out for a few seconds and then turned to face the two Special Agents. Composed ... he began to speak. "As you know, Steve Mason, your Ted Murphy, was a very good linguist and a damn fine Marine. He was Captain Ted Murphy until he joined Force Recon Co. He came to me before joining He served in Bosnia, Syria, and in the First Gulf War. You are probably more familiar with the name Operation Desert Storm, which was the name for the air and land military response in the First Gulf War, or The Iraq War. "

"Steve was assigned wherever he was needed. Because he spoke so many languages fluently and could write them as well, he was indispensable to us. But he wasn't limited to being a linguist. He was also a great negotiator between various foreign powers. In times of crisis, we used his expertise more than once. Well, something happened in early fall, 1989. Let me give you a little history. While still with the Marine's, in 1982, Ted joined Force Recon Co. "Two CIA operatives met with and recruited Ted in Peoria, Ill. 7 January, 82 while he was on a trip for 'Big Blue'. They coerced him in their usual manner to cooperate with them. We use the term coerced loosely, but literally no-one can be forced to join, they are only "persuaded with irrefutable justifications." As you already know, Lieutenant Colonel Nicki James, a U. S. Marine Analyst, and Major Matt McGuire were the two main contacts while he was with Force Recon Co. Captain Mason received his orders through Major McGuire and worked directly with him and Lieutenant Colonel James on several assignments. There was a third officer that met with Mason from time-to-time, but not with James or McGuire. I can't give you his name; it would jeopardize national security if it got out. When Mason joined the CIA, he was Mason's contact. The documents exchanged in those meetings were essential to Operative Mason's missions. Officially however none of the positions we've mentioned exist, and anything I say to you today I didn't say. You were never here and we never met. Agreed?" Kassidy and Trent said, "Yes, of course sir."

"Prior to Ted Murphy leaving the service in January of 1989, he had been involved in some pretty wieldy maneuvers in Bosnia, the Persian Gulf and Syria. What he saw was unperceivable to most people. His position as an interpreter gave him responsibility and authority. He was a medium of communication between the locals and the Americans. He was responsible for the lives of the Americans by teaching them what's right and what's wrong in the culture they were thrown into, and he interpreted communications between the enemy and the Americans. He was close to death frequently, but fortunately spared while thousands of other innocent people weren't. In 1976, after a bomb exploded outside a playground where thirty-two children were slaughtered he became bitter and withdrawn. He felt somehow that he was responsible, that he had said or done something that he shouldn't have. Soon after, in the fall of 1977, he came to me talking about retiring. We discussed at length his time in the service and his plans for the future. He said he would give retiring more thought. Two weeks later he came back to see me, but he was resolute in his decision to leave the service. I couldn't talk him out of it. The horror of what he had seen and had to deal with was too much for him. The loss of fellow soldiers was enough, but it was the genocide and crimes against humanity that forced him to retire. However, that was also part of the reason Ted Murphy, in 1978, was able to be influenced to join Force Recon Co. and serve his country again. However, he was determined, that to join Force Recon Co. meant he would have to change his name to protect his family. He said, "I have been threatened many times by people that I've had to deal with over the years. Joining Force Co., is more dangerous than my previous position and I open myself and my family up to even more threats." By changing my name, it will be more difficult for my enemies to find my family." It was then that he became Captain Steve Mason. He was a force to be reckoned with.

"I'm sure you are aware; wars are not always fought by fundamental principles set down in black-and-white. Things seemingly have gone wrong for the most part when we've tried to fight by modern rules. For example, the rules laid down in George Orwell's *Futuristic Nightmare,* where the three superpowers realign every few months; ... the good guys become bad guys and nobody ever wins or loses and the war never ends."

"Captain Mason was approached again, in 1988. This time it was by the CIA. They had two very specific assignments in mind for him. The first one involved an *unauthorized mission* to find any leads on a Bosnian Serb leader Radovan Karadzic. He was accused of war crimes, of plotting campaigns of ethnic cleansing and genocide to drive Muslims and Croats out of parts of Bosnia they believed should be attached to Serbia. He was also closely implicated in the abuses in Bosnia, and more recently of masterminding the deadly wartime siege of Sarajevo. While searching for him, Operative Mason said Karadzic used false names such as *Dragan Dabic* and applied many disguises. Mason was instrumental in providing us with a great deal of additional information on Karadzic which led to his capture." [3]

"Operative Mason's second assignment followed on the heels of Donald Rumsfeld's visit to Iran. It was prior to the cease-fire with Iran being signed in August of 1988. (Kuwait had been part of the Ottoman province of Basra, although the ruling dynasty, the al-Sabah family, had concluded a protectorate agreement in 1899 which assigned responsibility for its foreign affairs to Britain. It did not make any attempt to secede from the Ottoman Empire.) There were no mutual agreements on borders or access to the ocean. At this time Saddam Hussein was the Iraqi President and the U. S. took a neutral position on border disputes with Iraq and Kuwait. Operative Mason's assignment, involved the CIA director William Wagner and the Kuwaiti head of security, Brigadier Mubarek Al-Fahd. Director Wagner asked Operative Mason to join him because of his great negotiating skills. Brigadier Al-Fahd said there was some evidence of a CIA - Kuwaiti plot to destabilize Iraq economically and politically and Director Wagner wanted Operative Mason to help him sway Brigadier Al-Fahd's opinion. The CIA and Kuwait have described the meeting as successful. However, Mason's job was also to find evidence of the truth."

Colonel Marshall continued, "In the fall of 1989, Mason wanted to leave the CIA. When he came back to the states he said he was done. He had served his country and now wanted out. He wanted to spend time with his family. I told him to take some time, go home, be with your family and come back and see me in six months. That wasn't the end of it for Operative Mason. What happened in the summer of 1990 convinced him to stay."

In early July 1990, Iraq complained about Kuwait's behavior, such as not respecting OPEC quotas and driving down the price of oil, thus further hurting the Iraqi economy. The collapse in oil prices had a catastrophic impact on the Iraqi economy. The Iraqi government described it as a form of economic warfare, which it claimed was aggravated by Kuwait's *slant drilling* across the border into Iraq's Rumaila oil field. [4]

Iraq complained about Kuwait's behavior, and openly threatened to take military action. On July 23rd, the CIA reported that Iraq had moved 30,000 troops to the Iraq-Kuwait border, and the U.S. naval fleet in the Persian Gulf was placed on alert, the same day that Saddam Hussein appeared on Television and the Western hostage were seen as *human shields*. We believe Operative Mason was definitely involved in this. On the 25th, Saddam Hussein met with April Glaspie, an American ambassador, in Baghdad. According to an Iraqi transcript of that meeting, Glaspie told the Iraqi delegation, "We have no opinion on the Arab- Arab conflicts."On the 31st, negotiations between Iraq and Kuwait in Jeddah failed violently."[5]

Iraq launched an invasion by bombing Kuwait City, the Kuwaiti capital. This started the Iraq Kuwait War leading to a seven month Iraqi occupation of Kuwait. This subsequently led to direct military intervention by the U. S. led forces in the Gulf War. The main Iraqi thrust into Kuwait City was conducted by commandos deployed by helicopters and boats to attack the city from the sea, while other divisions seized the airports and two air bases. The Iraqi's assaulted the Dasman Emir of Kuwait. It was defended by the Emiri Guard and supported with M84 tanks. In the process, the Iraqis killed Sheikh Fahad. Kuwaiti Armed Forces were either overrun by the Iraqi Republican Guard, or had fled to neighboring Saudi Arabia. The Emir and key ministers were able to get out and head south along the highway for refuge in Saudi Arabia. Iraqi ground forces consolidated their control on Kuwait City, then headed south and redeployed along the border of Saudi Arabia. After the decisive Iraqi victory, Saddam Hussein installed his cousin, Ali Hassan al-Majid (Chemical Ali) as the governor of Kuwait.[6]

Out of fear the Iraqi army could launch an invasion of Saudi Arabia; U.S. President George H. W. Bush quickly announced that the U.S. would launch a *wholly defensive* mission to prevent Iraq from invading Saudi Arabia under the code name *Operation Desert Shield*. Operation Desert Shield began on 7 August, 1990 when U.S. troops were sent to Saudi Arabia due also to the request of its monarch, King Fahd, who had earlier called for U.S. military assistance. This "wholly defensive" doctrine was quickly abandoned when, on 8 August, Iraq declared Kuwait to be the 19th province of Iraq and Saddam Hussein named his cousin, Ali Hassan Al-Majid as its military-governor. It was then, "On 23 August, 1990 Saddam Hussein appeared on television with Western hostages to whom he had refused exit visas. They were seen as *human shields*, though Hussein denied the claim. Following this a secret US investigative group was formed." [7]

"Abhorring the human atrocities of war as Operative Mason did, I am sure that the thought of Saddam Hussein using *human shields* drove him to stay with the CIA.

"Mason became an integral influence in strengthening the CIA involvement in the Iraq War. To help you understand why, let me give you an idea of what drove the Iraq War & the CIA involvement."

Colonel Marshall summarizes the history as follows: The Iraq-Kuwait dispute involved Iraqi claim's to Kuwait as a territory of Iraq. After gaining independence from the United Kingdom in 1932, the Iraqi government immediately declared that Kuwait was rightfully a territory of Iraq, as it had been an Iraqi territory for centuries until the British creation of Kuwait after World War I. Iraq claimed Kuwait had been a part of the Ottoman Empire's province of Basra. Its ruling dynasty, the al-Sabah family, had concluded a protectorate agreement in 1899 that assigned responsibility for its foreign affairs to Britain. Britain drew the border between the two countries, and deliberately tried to limit Iraq's access to the ocean so that any future Iraqi government would be in no position to threaten Britain's domination of the Persian Gulf. Iraq refused to accept the border, and did not recognize the Kuwaiti government until 1963.

It was a war waged by a U.N. authorized coalition force from thirty-four nations led by the United States and United Kingdom, against Iraq. In a U.S. bid to open full diplomatic relations with Iraq, the country was removed from the U.S. list of State Sponsors of Terrorism.

Ostensibly this was because of improvement in the regime's record, although former United States Assistant Secretary of Defense Noel Koch later stated, "No one had any doubts about Iraqis' continued involvement in terrorism... The real reason was to help them succeed in the war against Iran."[8]

On 16 January, 1991 the conflict to expel Iraqi troops from Kuwait began with an aerial bombardment, followed by a ground assault on 2 February. This was a decisive victory for the coalition forces, which liberated Kuwait and the coalition advanced into Iraqi territory. Once they stopped their advance, they declared a cease-fire 100 hours after the ground campaign started. Aerial and ground combat by coalition forces (A United Nations Coalition Force included USA, Arab and European countries) were confined to Iraq, Kuwait, and areas on the border of Saudi Arabia. However, Iraq launched Scud missiles against military targets in Saudi Arabia and against Israel.

United Nations Security Council Resolution 665 followed soon after, which authorized a naval blockade to enforce the economic sanctions against Iraq. The resolution stated "*The use of measures commensurate to the specific circumstances as may be necessary ... to halt all inward and outward maritime shipping in order to inspect and verify their cargoes and destinations and to ensure strict implementation of resolution 661.*" [9]

From the beginning, U.S. officials insisted on a total Iraqi pullout from Kuwait, without any linkage to other Middle Eastern problems, fearing any concessions would strengthen Iraqi influence in the region for years to come.

One of the main concerns of the west was the significant threat Iraq posed to Saudi Arabia. Following the conquest of Kuwait, the Iraqi army was within easy striking distance of Saudi oil fields. Control of these fields, along with Kuwaiti and Iraqi reserves, would have given Hussein control over the majority of the world's oil reserves.

Soon after his conquest of Kuwait, Hussein began verbally attacking the Saudi kingdom. He argued, "The U.S. supported Saudi state was an illegitimate and unworthy guardian of the holy cities of Mecca and Medina." [10] This prompted the United States to take action.

I hope I have given you a clearer picture of the CIA involvement in the Iraqi War and what drove Operative Mason to join the CIA. Once he accomplished his covert mission in Iraq, he returned to the United States 15 May, 1991. This time he desperately wanted out of any more CIA assignments. He had completed his assignments with all the zeal, motivation, and responsibility any commander could hope for. God bless and keep him for that! Officially he was discharged from the military in August, 1991. In January of 1992, after the horrific death of Joyce and the kidnapping of Catherine, Ted showed back up at my office. He was insanely mad and wanted back into Force Recon Co. I told him he needed time to grieve, but he was insistent that he was ready. I told him that he needed to be evaluated and receive a release from our division Psych officer, Montgomery Weiss, Ph.D., before he could return to active duty. He left my office and I haven't heard from him since. However, we believe Mason may have become more involved in further CIA activities.

We searched for Mason for years since that last meeting with Nicki James in January, 1992. About six months ago, my contacts led me to believe that he may have been on a secret assignment, called COBRA-DEM. I haven't heard anything further. I have no idea what has happened to him.

What you decide to do from here on is up to you. Because I cared deeply for Mason, I'm going to give you a name of someone you may decide to contact. His name is Colonel Thomas Hunter. He was the lead on *COBRA-DEM*. Here is his phone number and where he can be reached. You may tell him I sent you, but again what was said in this room was never said.

This meeting is adjourned, but I will always be available to the both of you. Before you leave ... Please know that I was filled with pain and regret when I heard about the death of Joyce and the kidnapping of Catherine. I was deeply saddened. Wait just a minute ... I have a small box in my file cabinet. If you would take it to Catherine I would appreciate it. Mason left it stating that if he didn't return, he wanted Catherine to have it; but, he wanted me to hold it until she matured enough to understand the bigger picture. I believe she is old enough now."

Colonel Marshall went slowly to one of his file cabinets, unlocked it and removed a small box. Turning, he went over and handed the box to Kassidy. She nervously took the box without looking in it. She didn't quite know what to think. Then Colonel Marshall smiled and said, "Let me know the results of your search and give my regards to Colonel Hunter when you see him."

Kassidy and Trent thanked Colonel Marshall for being so gracious and for all of the information. They told him how much they appreciated his help, shook his hand, said goodbye, and slowly walked out the door. Kassidy tucked the box securely into her briefcase. She would give it to Catherine the next time she saw her.

Chapter 10

Closer to the Truth

Special Agent's Kassidy and Trent left Colonel Marshall and headed for Colonel Hunter's office in the NCIS Headquarters Building located on the same Marine Corps Base. They debated opening the box Lieutenant Colonel Marshall gave them, but decide not to. They felt that Catherine should be the one to open it.

Trent called ahead to Colonel Hunter's office. An aid met us at the main entrance to the building and escorted us to his office. Colonel Hunter greeted us by saying, "So get on with it, what brings your here?" We explained that we understood he was the lead on COBRA-DEM that we were searching for Steve Mason. He said, "... Well don't just stand there, have a seat and we'll talk. How do you know about *COBRA-DEM*? Never mind, I know you've been to see Colonel Marshall. He just called and informed me that he sent you here. To begin with I want you to know: Ted Murphy, aka Captain Mason was a damn good Marine, a loyal American, and a devout Christian, that I couldn't be more proud of. He worked for me on *COBRA-DEM*. I regret to say that he lost everything because of the war including his wife and family. Now, tell me, what is this all about? What do you want and how are you connected to Steve Mason?"

We related our story to him as succinctly as we could and ask for his help in finding Steve Mason.

Colonel Hunter said, "You need to understand that he served this country on many, many missions. He would complete one mission, go home for awhile on leave and come back and complete another mission as needed. Whether in the Marine's or in the CIA, his service to this country was invaluable. I can't tell you what *COBRA-DEM* is, but I will say that the last time I heard from Mason he was in Beirut. Don't mean to get off the topic, but if you've never been to Beirut, you can't imagine how beautiful it is. It was once a Mecca for the rich, but the Lebanese Civil War brought death and destruction to it, which virtually destroyed the country and it was a battleground for the forces of Hezbollah. Beirut became Lebanon's capital in 1943. It's the largest city of Lebanon, located on a peninsula at the midpoint of Lebanon's coastline with the Mediterranean.

Mason was there in 1983. Let me give you a little background regarding the area in Beirut where he was sent and the surrounding circumstances. It will help you appreciate just how dangerous his missions were. His first mission was the result of the Islamic Jihad claiming responsibility for the bombing of the American Marines barracks in Beirut, 23 October, 1983. It was a suicide truck bombing. The death toll was 241 American servicemen: 220 Marines, 18 Navy Seabees, 3 Army soldiers and 60 Americans were injured. It was the deadliest single-day death toll for US Marines since the Battle of Iwo Jima in WW II. About two minutes after the Marine Barracks bombing, a similar attack occurred against the barracks of the French 3rd Company of the 1st Parachute Chasseur Regiment. This was six kilometers away in the Ramlet al Barda of West Beirut. The suicide bomber drove his truck down a ramp in the 'Drakkar' building's underground parking garage and detonated his bomb leveling the eight-story building and killing 58 French Paratroopers and injuring 15 others. The ill will generated among Lebanese Muslims, especially from Shiites living in the slums of West Beirut and around the airport where the Marines were headquartered was considered a major motivation for the bombings. US troops were seen to side with the Maronite Catholics in their dominating of Lebanon which exacerbated adverse Muslim feelings against Americans presence. This was intensified when missiles lobbed by the U. S. Sixth Fleet hit innocent by-standers in the Druze-dominated Shuf Mountains.[11]

Some analysts believe the Islamic Republic of Iran was heavily involved and that a major factor leading it to participate in the attacks on the barracks was America's support for Iraq in the Iran-Iraq War and its extending of $2.5 billion in trade credit to Iraq while halting the shipments of arms to Iran. [12]A few weeks before the bombing, Iran warned that providing armaments to Iran's enemies would provoke retaliatory punishment.

During this time Mason's task was instrumental in locating and communicating crucial information. Col. Timothy J. Geroghty, the Commander of the Marines in Beirut at the time of the incident, said "The Marine and French headquarters were targeted primarily because of who we were and what we represented." U. S. President Ronald Reagan called the attack a "despicable act" and pledged to keep a military force in Lebanon."[13] Mason went home on leave following the completion of his task.

Hezbollah (meaning "Party of God") is a Shi'a Muslim militant group and political party based in Lebanon that mobilized a resistance movement throughout much of the Arab and Muslim worlds. The movement is seen as the sacred Muslim struggle against foreign occupation. It receives financial and political support from Iran and Syria. The 1983 report by the U.S. Department of Defense Commission's on the Marine barrack's attack recommended that the National Security Council re-examine alternative ways to reach "American objectives in Lebanon." U. S. Marines were moved offshore where they could not be targeted. On 7 February, 1984, President Regan ordered the Marines to begin withdrawing from Lebanon. This was completed on 26 February. The rest were withdrawn by April, 1984. On 8 February, 1984 the USS New Jersey fired about 300 shells at Druze and Syrian positions in the Bekaa Valley East of Beirut. Some 30 of these massive projectiles rained down on a Syrian Command Post, allegedly killing the General who commanded the Syrian forces in Lebanon and several other senior officers. In his memoir, General Colin Powell noted that, "When the shells started falling on the Shiites, they assumed the American *referee* had taken sides." He also said, "... It is noteworthy that the United States provided direct naval gunfire support for a week to the Lebanese Army at a mountain village called Suq-al-Garb. I strongly opposed it. The French conducted an air strike on 23 September in the <u>Bekaa Valley</u>. American support removed any lingering doubts of our neutrality, and I stated to my staff at the time that we were going to pay in blood for this decision."[14]

January, 1992, was Mason's last mission to Beirut. Captain Christopher Taylor, a Military Attaché out of the Beirut Embassy, presented me with a story so crazy that I felt it might actually be true. Taylor said that he didn't know who ordered Mason on the mission or what the mission was. Since the War ended in 1989, it was doubtful that his mission involved anything to do with the war. However, tensions between the Muslim West and the Christian East still remained. Having talked to Mason, Taylor sensed that the mission may have involved something personal. Taylor said, "Several things seemed strange or unusual for Mason and they caught my attention. First, he was dressed in an old fashioned long military trench coat over camouflage field pants and shirt. His boots were heavy work boots and he had a duffel bag and back pack fully loaded. It appeared that he had enough supplies to last him for quite a while. During normal missions, he's dressed in regular uniforms or fatigues, and carried minimal supplies. Second, I ask him if he needed me to fill out any paperwork for him. Usually he does. This time he said 'No, this is a very important covert mission to locate three insurgents. I have to do it alone and I will complete it or die trying. Just to give you a little heads up, I'm heading to Tripoli and then on to Homs (Hims), Syria. If I haven't found who I'm looking for by then I will be heading east to Tiyas, then to Tadmur, Palmyra and maybe on to As Sukhnah looking for them. I'm sure I will have found all of them by then.' Third, I ask him when I would see him again and if he would be bringing captives back with him and he said, 'If I'm not back in a month, I'll have either been captured or killed, so I guess if neither of those have happened. ... Yes, I am confident you will be seeing me again. As to whether or not I will be bringing back captives ... I hope not. I intend to be their judge, jury and executioner. ... On second thought, if I'm not back in a month, you can deliver a letter to Colonel Hunter in the NCIS Headquarters in Virginia for me. He pulled a sealed letter out of his backpack and handed it to me. Under normal circumstances, he would file a plan with me in case he needed backup. If he needed backup he would contact me; I would notify Colonel Hunter and we would send help. Well this time ... he didn't contact me and he wasn't back in a month. All I could do was to take his letter out of the file and forward it on to Colonel Hunter as he had asked."

Colonel Hunter told us that he had received the letter on 5 February, 1992. He related the following: As you probably realize, I can't let you see the letter, but in the letter Mason related to me who he felt the insurgents were, where he was headed and why. This was definitely a personal mission having to do with the death of his wife Joyce and the kidnapping of his daughter, Catherine. His first mission to Beirut was a covert investigation involving a specific small group of Druze and Syrian forces. This small group of Druze activists disputed Mason's claims and threatened force, to get Mason to back-off and retract his report. When Operative Mason refused, the threats became more severe.

Mason's reports involved Syrian forces on their way back to Syria from Lebanon where about 100 soldiers, including several officers were killed. Several civilian workers were also killed in an ambush by armed terrorist groups on the Damascus-Homs highway. Mason was sent into Lebanon and Syria to investigate the bombing of Marines, prior to the European Union imposing sanctions on Syrian officials and charges against Druze and Syrian forces. SANA, the state-run news agency was pursuing *armed terrorist groups* in response to Mason's investigation, acting on information he had given them. Prior to his return to Beirut in 1990, Operative Mason got information from SANA regarding the group's location and recent activities. According to his letter, Operative Mason said he was positive that Ammar Rami-Abdul, along with Ammar's closest ally, Bashar al Hussein, and a female, Lamia al-Sabah, were responsible for the hit on Joyce and for Catherine's kidnapping. He felt that the three of them were determined to send him a message. Mason undertook this mission to exact revenge or to bring them to justice no-matter-what. Officially we could not send troops in to help Mason, nor to find him. However, under-the-radar, I did send in a small group to find information as to Mason's whereabouts. My men were led to believe that Mason may be held captive in Tadmur Military Prison. However, their sources were unable to positively confirm or deny that.

At the present time I don't know whether Mason is or has been held there, but we have reason to believe he was a prisoner there in 1992. At that time, no-one was allowed in the prison to look at records or search for anyone. I can let you read the report that I obtained from Amnesty International on the state of prisoners in the Tadmur (Tadmor) Military Prison.

Colonel Hunter handed the Amnesty International report to Trent. It stated the following: "For over two decades Amnesty International has documented and campaigned on a range of serious human rights violations in Syria, including the arbitrary detention of political opponents, the long-term detention of prisoners of conscience, torture and ill-treatment, and political killings. Under the state of emergency, which has remained in force without interruption since 8 March, 1963, different branches of the security forces have been able to arbitrarily detain political suspects at will for as long as they please. Tens of thousands of people have been rounded up in successive waves of mass arrests targeted at suspected members of left-wing, Islamist or Arab nationalist organizations or Kurdish political groups, or at anyone engaged in activities opposed to the government and its policies. Among those arrested were hundreds of prisoners of conscience. Those detained have frequently been tortured while held in total isolation from the outside world for months or years without charge or trial. Many thousands of families have been kept in the dark about the fate of their relatives. Some, whose loved ones "disappeared" after arrest, fear the worst. Since the beginning of the 1990's, the majority of political prisoners in Syria have been released in batches by presidential amnesties, or on expiry of their prison terms. The most recent of these amnesties was issued by President Bashar al-Assad in November, 2000 and reportedly covered 600 political prisoners from various opposition groups. Since 1991, when the first amnesty was declared, the number of political prisoners, including *prisoners of conscience*, has been reduced from several thousand to hundreds. Despite numerous allegations of torture, some of which were made in court by the victims themselves, no proper investigations appear to have been carried out by the Syrian authorities. Torture has been used as a means of extracting information and also as a form of punishment. In a report published in the April, 1995 Amnesty International stated that most of the 500 or more defendants tried before the Supreme State Security Court since July, 1992 had testified in court that they had been tortured. None were known to have been medically examined and no investigations were known to have been carried out. In March, 1997 the Minister of the Interior informed Amnesty International delegates that any official who committed torture or ill-treatment would be brought to court. He also stated that any person who suffered torture had the right to make a complaint to a judge who would then refer the case to the Ministry of the Interior so that the necessary measures could be taken. However, the torture allegations presented by Amnesty International to the Syrian authorities remain unanswered. No investigations into these cases are known to have been carried out. A report smuggled out in 1999, to Amnesty International by a group of former Syrian prisoners referred to the situation in Tadmur Prison as follows: "When death is a daily occurrence, lurking in torture, random beatings, eye-gouging, broken limbs and crushed fingers, ... when death stares you in the face and is only avoided by sheer chance ... wouldn't you welcome the merciful release of a bullet." This is reported to be the case in Tadmur Prison where between 600 and 700 political prisoners are currently believed to be held.[15]

Because of Mason's presence in Tadmur while searching for the insurgents, he may have said or done something that could have been construed as opposition to Syria's government policies. If so, he could have been one of those hundreds of *prisoners of conscience* arrested.

The Tadmur Military Prison is located in the Homs desert, approximately 250 km northeast of Damascus. It was built initially as a military barracks by the French Mandate authorities in Syria (1920-1946). Subsequently it was apparently used as a prison for military personnel accused of ordinary criminal offences. It appears that the authorities chose Tadmur because its remote location and harsh regime allow political prisoners to be completely cut off from the outside world while they are being tortured and ill-treated. From the early 1970's Tadmur Prison began to be used to hold political prisoners who were kept in complete isolation from the outside world, but mostly for just a matter of months. At that time transport was very difficult, making it almost impossible for families to visit relatives sent to

Tadmur Prison. The prison is under the administration of the military police, a security force responsible to the Ministry of Defense, and was said to be guarded by a force of the Special Units. As a military prison, Tadmur does not fall under the supervision of the Ministry of Justice which inspects civilian prisons." [16]

After reading the report, Kassidy and Trent asked Colonel Hunter, "What can we do now to find Mason ... and do you know of anyone we can contact to find out if he's at Tadmur Military Prison?" After a long pensive pause, he responded, "Give me some time to check into things and I'll get back with you."

Chapter *11*

Hope Justified

Kassidy and Trent brought Todd Taylor, Clyde Duncan, James Walker, and Carrie Wagner up-to-speed on the investigation so far.

Three days later, Kassidy and Trent received a message from Colonel Hunter to meet back with him at the MCB (Marine Corps Base), Quantico, Virginia.

Kassidy and Trent arrive at the MCB, Quantico, with heightened excitement, yet with some dread. They anguished that Colonel Hunter might say their quest was finished. They were met at the gate and ushered to his office.

Colonel Hunter said, "I hope you're ready for this. Please take a seat."They were really nervous. "I want you to realize that while Murphy was a Captain for the Marine's and later became Mason with Force Recon Co. he was only one of millions of super fine Marine's. These are great men who give all they've got, even their lives, supporting our country every day. Each Marine is as special as the next to our military and to this country. I have thought long and hard about just how we can help you, and I must admit I almost said, forget it. But …I couldn't in good conscience just give up on trying to find Mason. I'm sure you must have heard the saying, *Once a Marine, always a Marine.* Well, he's not only a super fine Marine; he has been a good friend to many of us here at MCB, Quantico for many years. Though he went on to join the CIA, he's always going to be a part of us here at Quantico. So … I have formed a small group of CID (US Marine Corps Criminal Investigation Division) personnel to work with us on a special mission to Syria, specifically to find Mason. Now … understand that this is going to take time. Captain Christopher Taylor will be leading the team under my direct supervision. It's important that we plan and organize our mission carefully. And … it has to be covert just as Mason's was, so I'm not going to explain our every move to you. You are going to have to be patient and trust that we will succeed in our mission."

Colonel Hunter said, "Now, It's time for you to leave. I will from time-to-time update you on our progress."

Kassidy and Trent thanked Colonel Hunter, shook his hand and left. Still primed with excitement they headed back to Albany and would tie-in with the team. They left James Walker a very brief message to tie-in, before heading to the airport.

Kassidy said to Trent, "Do you think our hope is justified?" "Yes," Trent responded, "I think we can legitimately have hope since the CID group has been commissioned to find Steve (Ted). You do realize that Colonel Hunter would not have formed the CID team if he wasn't pretty certain that it would be a success one way or the other." We both smiled and felt relieved to know we had done all we could to help Catherine and Chris find their father or to at least have closure in knowing what happened to him. Kassidy still beaming with excitement said, "Can you just imagine what Catherine and Grandmother Alice are going to do when we tell them. Oh … I almost forgot. I have that box for Catherine that Colonel Marshall gave us. Let's go back to Albany, tie in with the rest of our team, take a day or two to wrap up loose ends at the office, and then visit Catherine and Grandmother

Alice in New York. What do you think Trent?" "That sounds good to me, Kas."

A couple of hours later, Kassidy and Trent landed in Albany. Pretty exhausted, they both went home to catch up on the usual chores, read their stacks of mail and relax for an evening. Bright and early the next morning, about 5:30 am, they decided to meet for breakfast and head for the office. When they got there everyone was buzzing with hyped energy and excitement. Trent asked James Walker what was going on, "What did we miss?" James Walker said, "This morning when we got here, there was a fax waiting for us from Colonel Hunter asking us to call him at Quantico. It looked urgent so I called him right away. He asked if either of you were here. I said you were both on your way in, you would be here shortly." Colonel Hunter said, "Tell them the mission's a Go! The team is flying to Syria this morning. They expect to meet with our consulate there and complete their final plans tomorrow afternoon at the latest." Trent and Kassidy both said, "That's great news." They couldn't believe how quickly Colonel Hunter's team had mobilized. Thinking about quickly, brought to mind our Special Agent's progress. Kassidy said, "Do you realize, Trent ... we were called into this investigation the first week of June and this is now only September thirtieth? Normally cases like this can take at least a year and sometimes more, to show progress like this. However ... we still have a long way to go, don't we? Who knows how long it will take the CID team to complete their mission. Trent agreed and said, "Let's spend the rest of the day finishing up some open-ended projects piled on our desks."

The morning finds our detectives having a leisurely breakfast. Trent's phone rings. It's Sheriff Montgomery. He said, "I was told that you and S. A. Kassidy Barnes were assigned to head up the special task force and I've found something that I'm sure you will need to look at. Shall I send it to you or would you like to come and pick it up?" Trent said, "Actually Kassidy and I have already planned to come to Vestal today to visit Alice and Catherine Murphy, so we will stop by your office first."

Trent and Kassidy headed by car for Vestal. They had already talked to Grandmother Alice to let her they were coming. She told them that Catherine would be home from work about 5:30 pm.

Trent and Kassidy arrived in Vestal, about 3:30 pm Wednesday afternoon, September 4th. The weather was beautiful. The sky was clear and the temperature was about 75 degrees. The trip had been fine so far and they were in good spirits. They stopped for a light snack and then headed to the sheriff's office. They introduced themselves and Sheriff Montgomery said, "I'm glad to meet you both. S. A. James Walker and S. A. Carrie Wagner told me you would be a great asset to the task force. Let me show you the reason I called you this morning." He went over and picked and envelope off of his desk. He said, "I was reorganizing my files and found a piece of evidence that was part of the original investigation. Apparently it had fallen down behind one of the drawers in my file cabinet. During the investigation in 1992 while my men and I were searching the barn, my flashlight caught just a glimmer of something shiny. I took a closer look and found this coin almost buried in the straw next to the wagon wheel. It looked like it was made of nickel. When I got back to the office, I did a little research on it and found out it was a 10 Syrian Pound with an Eagle on it. The records show that in 1960, those coins were made of cupro-nickel. With a magnifier I could see a couple partial finger prints on it. I put the coin in the envelope and placed it in the file thinking I wanted to look more at it later, and then forgot about it. I can release it to you for further investigation." With zero hesitation we agreed to take it. Trent said, "Fantastic! This may be the most definitive lead we've had." We ask Sheriff Montgomery if he had any other news for us, and he said "No." We thanked him and told him we would keep in touch.

It was about 5:30 pm and we headed for Alice and Catherine's. Catherine was home when we got there and very eager and excited to see us. She and Grandmother Alice invited us in and offered us some ice-tea. After we talked for a little while I took the box from my purse and handed it to Catherine. Trent and I then explained how Colonel Dave Marshall had given it to us to bring to her and that it was from her father. She began to shake a little as she cut the string it was tied with. Inside she found a gold medallion necklace. As she carefully lifted it out of the box, you could see a tear running down her cheek. On the front of the medallion were two angels, hands touching arched over a little girl and a baby. Above the angels were the names Catherine and Chris and below the little girl and baby were the words, Love Daddy. On the back were the signs of the four elements: water, fire, earth, and air. Upon seeing this Grandmother Alice started to cry. She said, "Ted gave this to Joyce when Chris was born. He must have added the 'Love Daddy' sometime after he left here." It was about the size of a silver-dollar, but the gold chain that it was on looked very delicate. There was a letter folded up in the bottom of the box. Catherine took it out very slowly and carefully opened it up. She sat down, read the letter, closed it up and stared at us, opened it up, read it once more and started to cry again. We all wanted to know what the letter said, but we didn't want to presume that she would want to share its contents with us. She looked at her grandmother as if to ask for permission to speak. Grandmother Alice smiled and said, "Go ahead dear."

Catherine turned to us and with her voice quivering said, "I can't read it to you right now, but if you would like to … you may read it." She handed the letter to Trent. He reached out and ever so gently took it from her. Both Trent and I sat down and read the letter together. When we were finished, I handed it to Grandmother Alice. The letter said, "Catherine, if you are reading this, I most likely will not be coming home, I'm sorry that I left you, but I had to avenge your mother's death and your kidnapping. I'm sure I know who was responsible. They threatened my life more than once. I wouldn't give in to them, but I never considered the thought that they would discover my real name and attack my family. I vowed to find them and bring them to justice. Catherine, I love you, your brother Chris, your mother Joyce and Grandmother Alice more than life itself. Please share this letter with the rest of the family. God willing, I will return home some day. I took the necklace from Joyce after she was shot. I felt that having it would give me strength and it would make me feel close to all of you while I was gone. Catherine, I know your mother would want you to have it. Do you remember how important the four elements and four seasons were to Grandfather Edwin? How they were carved into the woodwork of the house. … I'm sure Grandfather Edwin has talked to you about them. He felt that they were all influenced by the energy of both love and strife, that we have to have both in our life to appreciate what God has given us. I know you have all suffered so much loss, but you are also loved so very much. Catherine, I can only hope that the angles are watching over you and Chris just as they are on the front of the medallion. The letter was signed, "With all my love to my beautiful princess, my son, and my mother."

When we all finished drying our tears, we told Catherine there was still hope for either finding her father or for getting closure. We explained what we had found out from Colonel Hunter regarding the mission with the CID team. She just ran up and threw her arms around us in a big group hug and said, "I love all of you!" She said, "Grandmother Alice has always been here for me and I love her so very much, but for seventeen years there was just a big empty feeling that haunted me. Now I have a brother and the possibility for finding out what happened to my father. I am so overjoyed. You have given me fantastic news and the most wonderful gift from my father. Now we can all hope.

Thank you so much. I will call my brother Chris tomorrow and tell him the wonderful news."

As they said their good-byes and were walking off the porch, Trent said, "When we hear anything from the CID team or Colonel Hunter, we will be sure to let you know as soon as possible." Catherine said, "Thank you so much." Kassidy stopped and took a deep breath and said, "What a gorgeous evening this is. The nice fresh country crisp air is invigorating. I almost wish I could spend more time here."Trent said, "I understand." A few hours later they were back home.

The next morning, Catherine called her brother Chris in Arizona. He answered the phone and was very excited to hear his sister's voice. Catherine told him what Trent and Kassidy had told her. She explained to him about their mother's medallion and the letter their dad had included in the box. There was silence for a few seconds on the other end of the phone. After he grasped what she was saying, he said to Catherine, "Do you really think that after all these years there might be the slightest possibility of them finding our father?" She said, "I'm praying for it and hoping." Chris said, "I'm sorry sis, I'm stunned. I really don't know what to think. I'm excited and scared at the same time. Can I come and spend some time with you and get out of the heat. You realize the temperature here is 90 degrees today." Catherine said, "I definitely want you to come and I'm sure Grandmother Alice will love having you here too." Check with Aunt Sarah and Uncle Tony and call me back."

It was only about an hour and Chris called Catherine back and said, "Mom said she will get the ticket today. You have to know that I still consider her my mom and Tony my dad. That's all I knew until you came out here after graduation." Catherine said, "Of course ... they are still your mom and dad. They adopted you. Grandmother Alice was like a mom to me for seventeen years. Our love for them will never change. I have just a few memories of our real mom, but I will never forget her. If we could have our birth dad back wouldn't you want to get to know him?" Chris said, "Of course, but I'm afraid that he won't know me or want me". Catherine reassured him. "Yes he will, Chris. I told you about the medallion. The angels were over both you and me. Dad hoped that God would see to it that he would someday return to us and that the angels would take care of us until then." Chris said, "I understand what you're saying Catherine, but I'm still scared and nervous about it. I think being with you and Grandmother Alice will help. Mom got my ticket for the day after tomorrow. How's that, sis?" "Great, I'm excited," said Catherine, "See you soon. I've got to go and tell Grandmother the good news."

It was late afternoon when Chris landed at the Broome County Airport. Grandmother Alice and Catherine were there to meet him. On the way back to the farm, Chris said, "This is fantastic, the air is so nice and cool. I've never seen leaves like that. The colors are beautiful. I'm so happy to be here with the both of you." Grandmother Alice said, "It's great to have you here Chris and you are welcome to stay here as long as you like. Of course, that's with your Joyce's permission." When they got back to the farm and entered the house, Chris said, "Grandmother Alice what is that, something smells so great?" Grandmother said, "Oh that's just dinner cooking." She had baked an apple pie this morning and had dinner cooking in the crock pot.

Chapter 12

The Road Less Traveled
to Discovery

The next morning after leaving the Murphy's, Trent and Kassidy went to their FBI Office in Albany. Their desks were overflowing with unfinished work. Trent said, "We weren't gone that long, how could our work pile up that fast. Oh well, we have to prioritize. First- things-first, we need to check the prints on that Syrian Pound. Then we can tackle the mounds of paperwork later." They proceeded to their lab where their technicians photographed and lifted the two visible prints, the one's Sheriff Montgomery had seen. They also used a Cyanoacrylate Fuming Chamber to isolate any latent prints. Sure enough, they now have found four distinctly different partial prints. Next they would scan the prints they found into AFIS (Automated Fingerprint identification System).[17]

If our two special agents were unable to find a match through AFIS, another source is available to them. Since our coin is Syrian currency our detectives could contact Interpol'. Interpol' is the World's Largest International Criminal Police Organization or ICPO with 188 member countries created in 1923. It gives rapid access to officially controlled information and facilitates

International police cooperation between countries to prevent or combat international crimes. It also assists US law enforcement in arrests.[18]

Another fingerprinting resource is available to the FBI called CODIS. They can do DNA fingerprinting, but a different sample such as skin or blood is necessary. The main advantage to this type of fingerprinting is that conventional fingerprints occur only on the fingertips, and are capable of being altered, but a DNA fingerprint is the same for every cell in the body and incapable of being altered.

Another resource available for the FBI, that Trent McGuire and Kassidy Barnes used earlier in their search for Operative Mason, is the NCIC, FBI's computerized National Crime Information Center (launched 27-Jan-67). It's a criminal database maintained by the FBI that holds a lot of information including missing and unidentified persons among other things.

Kassidy and Trent worked together with their resources and found that one of the partial prints matched a print from Matt McGuire. They both looked at each other with a look of amazement. They wondered: Could that possibly be the same Major Matt McGuire that met Mason at the Pub in Peoria? Why would his print be on a Syrian coin? Trent said, "We have to find answers,"They had to go through Interpol for the second partial print and found a match to Ammar Rami-Abdul. He had multiple arrests for his involvement with political rioting in Lebanon and Syria and he was charged with heading an anti-Christian uprising in Beirut in 1983. This was the name of one of the three people that had threatened Mason. Trent contacted Interpol' to request their assistance in locating Ammar Rami-Abdul. While he was doing that, Kassidy contacted NCIS to ask for their assistance in locating Major Matt McGuire and also gave his name to Interpol', in case he had been involved in any subversive activities in Libya or Syria for example.

With an air of excitement, Kassidy said, "Piece-by-piece our case seems to be coming together." She faxed the information that we found back to Sheriff Montgomery and to Colonel Hunter.

Three weeks passed. There were no messages for our special agents from Interpol, NCIS, the CID team or from Colonel Hunter. Trent and Kassidy began to show concern. Their general good natured banter was less-and-less.

Kassidy said to Trent, "I just realized something ironic, that Major Matt McGuire and you have the same last name." Trent said, "So what?" "Well do you have any relatives in your family tree by the name of Matt McGuire?" Trent said, "You've got to be kidding, no ... not that I know of." Kassidy continued, "Have you ever looked into your lineage, or family tree." "No," said Trent. "Well", Kas said, "We need to fix that."

They both left work and decided to grab a bite to eat before heading home. It's convenient for them to ride back and forth to work together since they only live two miles apart. They both seemed kind of quiet and a little down at dinner. Trent said to Kassidy, "What's bothering you?" She said, "Not much, I'm just concerned that we haven't heard anything more about our case." He said, "I'm sure we will hear something soon, don't worry about it." "Well", she said ... "Let's forget about it for tonight. What are you up to after dinner?" He said, "Nothing, how about you?" She said, "Why not come over to my place and we can relax and watch a movie or play a board game or something." "Sure, Why not?" he said, so they finished dinner and headed to Kassidy's apartment.

Kassidy fixed them both a drink. "Hey, I have a great idea", she said as she powered up her lap top. "Let's find out where you came from". He laughed. She said, "Silly, I'm talking about your family history, your genealogy." "Yeah right," said Trent. "No, I'm serious," said Kassidy. "Oh, alright," he said. They both had their drinks in hand and pulled up a chair to the desk. After going to a genealogy website, Kas said, "Since we did a background check on Matt McGuire today, we know his parents names were Isabel and Walter McGuire. Let's see if any of your relative's names match those. All of a sudden it was there, they found a Matt McGuire, a son of his father's cousin, Walter McGuire, married to Isabel. Trent said, "This is surreal Kass, how can it be? This all seems so absurd, that I could possibly have a relative involved in an investigation that we were working on. How bizarre is that? I know we need to check it out, but I'm still amazed. I'll think about it overnight and we can proceed from there in the morning. I need to go home and get some sleep. Thanks for your help Kass and have a good night. I will pick you up around six in the morning and we can go for a quick breakfast before work. How does that sound?" Kassidy said, "Great. See you in the morning."

Chapter 13

On The Brink

Kassidy woke up early, about 4:30 am and restlessly moved about her apartment straightening things up before getting ready for Trent to pick her up for breakfast. She couldn't help worrying about why they hadn't received any news from Interpol, NCIS or from their CID group in Syria. She thought possibly 'no-news-is-good-news', but she wasn't satisfied to leave it at that. She decided that the first thing they would do when they got to the office would be to contact Interpol and then try to reach anyone in Colonel Hunter's office to see if they had received any new information.

Trent knocked on her door; he was right on-time to pick her up for work. "Be right there," Kassidy shouted. It was a beautiful cool, morning. They went for breakfast at the corner coffee shop nearby, but didn't talk much. Both had all kinds of thoughts running through their mind. Kassidy said, "What do you want to do first when we get to work." Trent said, "I've been thinking a lot about Matt McGuire, but it's more important that we contact Interpol, NCIS and Colonel Hunter's office first." "Absolutely," Kassidy said. They were at work by 6:45 am.

Trent and Kassidy's contact at Interpol told them that their last known location of Ammar Rami-Abdul[19] was in the central city of Homs and that their sources placed him in the town of Rastan as of a month ago. The only information they had on Major Matt McGuire was an involvement with a Lamia al-Sabah in 1983. They were arrested together for questioning in an uprising with Lebanese Muslims. They had Matt McGuire working with Colonel Timothy J. Geraghty, (pronounced with a silent gh, Geraty) the commander of the Marines in Beirut prior to this incident. They said they had no record of him after that. We thanked them for their information.

Special Agent Harris at NCIS told us that Major Matt McGuire was last assigned in Beirut in 1983 to work with Lieutenant Colonel Nicki James, the U. S. Marine Intelligence Analyst, on a special investigation.

We now know that Ammar Rami-Abdul, Lamia al-Sabah, Major Matt McGuire, Lieutenant Colonel Nicki James, and Steve Mason are all involved somehow, but just how we have no clue. We think that the other person Mason mentioned in his letter to Colonel Hunter, Bashar al Hussein al Hussein (Ammar Rami-Abdul's ally), is also involved.

We asked Special Agent Harris to keep looking into Major Matt McGuire's involvement and to keep us posted. He told us that Syrian authorities had confirmed that Mason had been arrested and taken to the Tadmur military prison along with 110 anti-government demonstrators in 1992.

Two more days went by and we finally heard from Colonel Hunter. He said they found out that Mason had been imprisoned in the 'Tadmur Military Prison', but that he was released along with 300 other prisoners by a Presidential Amnesty from President Bashar Assad a week ago. The CID group found that he was last seen in the town of Talbiseh as recent as three days ago. The group was told that he was searching for Ammar Rami-Abdul and the other two. They said he was heading for Teir Maaleh a nearby town.

Trent and Kassidy's excitement was immeasurable; to know that as of last week Ted (Steve Mason) may still be alive. Colonel Hunter said that his men were close to finding Mason and that he would keep them posted as the search played out.

The next day Trent got the call. They had found Mason in Ar Raqqa, a city on the North bank of the Euphrates. He was in the Fisherman Wharf Hotel with Ammar Rami-Abdul, and Bashar al Hussein. The CID group had come in just in time. They feared that Mason may have executed Ammar Rami-Abdul and Bashar al Hussein already. They were pleasantly surprised to find them both still alive. Under interrogation, Bashar al Hussein told them he had last met Lamia al-Sabah in Homs. Part of the CID team took the two insurgents into custody for the killing and kidnapping. Two more of the CID team went to Homs to locate her. Their intel was correct, the CID officers took her into custody. Mason was in extremely bad shape. The other two members of the CID team, along with Colonel Hunter were to accompany Mason on a plane back to the Navy Medical Center in Portsmouth, Virginia.

Colonel Hunter notified the members of the special *task force* immediately upon Mason's return to the United States. Trent and Kassidy went to visit Alice and Catherine Murphy to tell them the good news in person.

When Grandmother Alice opened the door, Kassidy said, "We have the greatest news, the CID group found Ted in Syria, he had been in prison since 1992 and is in pretty bad shape, but he's alive and now he's back in the United States." Grandmother Alice screamed, "Catherine and Chris come here, you've got to hear this." Kassidy repeated it for Catherine and Chris, and then said, "He's in the Navy Medical Center in Portsmouth, Virginia." Catherine said, "When can we see him?" Kassidy said, "After his condition is stabilized, he will have to be debriefed by Colonel Hunter's team. Then when he is able to be moved, they will bring him back to New York, you can see him then."

After three days of medical examination and treatment, Colonel Hunter met with Mason to determine what exactly happened to him after he left the U.S. Embassy in Beirut.

Mason tells this story to Colonel Hunter: "After leaving the embassy in Beirut I searched for Ammar Rami-Abdul, Bashar al Hussein and Lamia al Hussein for two weeks. I needed some supplies so I stopped at a market in Sanaa. A small group of rights activists had gathered nearby when an uprising broke out. There was a lot of commotion. I saw a mother trying to comfort her little girl who had been injured. I went to the mother to see if I could be of help. She said her daughter couldn't breathe and that her leg was broken. I gave the little girl CPR and she started breathing. I picked her up to move her out of the crowd to a safe area where I could set her leg. However, the crowd started pushing and shoving and closed in on us. I couldn't go anywhere; I was caught in the middle of it. Residents had formed a human chain to keep soldiers away to no avail. Some of the soldiers defected. I had met one of the soldiers before when I was on my first mission to Beirut. At that time we became friends. He gave me some information about Ammar Rami-Abdul's activity in Syria in the past, and vowed to help me again if at all possible. The soldier, Sabeen al Hussein, said he was sorry that he couldn't keep me from being arrested, but he would try to contact me later in prison.

I was arrested with the group of activists and taken to the Tadmur Prison. Sabeen smuggled information in to me from time-to-time. It was always a ray of hope. It fostered within me, the will to live. I would think of my wife Joyce, how she died and wondered about the welfare of my two beautiful children. I was confident that my mother and father would take good care of them, but it had been so very, very long since I had seen them. I longed to hold them in my arms again. I dreamt of the day when I would again see their smiling faces. It kept me from going crazy. I thought, "Inwardly I may never heal ... my Joyce is gone ... my children are away from me ... I'm stuck in here for what seems like an eternity, not knowing from day-to-day if I will live to see my family again." I survived the barbaric beatings and vicious brutality that I experienced in prison every day by focusing on two things: First, I focused on my family ... the love I had for them. I imagined their faces ... the sound of their voices ... every birthday and every holiday. Second, I focused on what I would do to the people that were behind the senseless death of Joyce and the kidnapping of Catherine. At the time I didn't know what I would say or do to them, but I knew I wanted justice. They needed to pay. I hoped and prayed every day for strength to survive ... that somehow, someday I would be able to get out of that prison and avenge my loss. Only then would I be able to face my children ... Knowing that I exacted justice on those who killed their mother. It was a shock, but a pleasant shock when I was released with a Presidential Amnesty from "President Bashar al-Assad." I couldn't believe it, I was finally freed. Sabeen al Hussein had kept me posted on the location of Ammar and Bashar. When I left the prison, to my surprise, Sabeen was waiting outside. In my physical condition it was difficult for me to walk, but I knew I had to complete my mission. He took me to the nearest town, As Sukhnah, where I received urgent care, food, and water. The next morning Sabeen helped me pursue Ammar and Bashar as far as Ar Rasafah. He gave me some currency, supplies, and an address in Ar Raqqa. We hugged; he wished me well and we said goodbye. From there I traveled alone by bus to Ar Raqqa, where you found me. Now, thank you God; with all of them arrested, justice will be mine. However, I won't be able to rest until they are convicted. My mission accomplished, I can now heal and get back with my loved ones.

Colonel Hunter said, "Mason, I still have some questions for you. A Syrian coin was found in the barn where Joyce was killed. Can you tell me why it would be there, or where it came from?" Mason said, "No, I have no idea why it was there or where it came from." "Well", Colonel Hunter said, "It had two different fingerprints on it, one was that of Ammar Rami-Abdul and the other was that of Major Matt McGuire. What can you tell me about any connection between those two?" Mason said, "Last I heard, Major McGuire was on assignment for Colonel Geraghty in Beirut, around 1983, I know nothing about a connection between him and Ammar Rami-Abdul. What aren't you telling me Colonel Hunter?"

Colonel Hunter said, "We know there was an involvement between Major McGuire and Lamia al-Sabah in 1983. They were arrested together for questioning in an uprising with Lebanese Muslims." Colonel Hunter asked Mason, "Why do you think they were together?" Mason said, "I really don't know. ... Matt McGuire and I have been friends for twenty-five years. I can't imagine that he would be involved in anything having to do with your investigation. However Colonel, I too would like to know the answer to why they were together and why his prints were on that coin. Please let me know the results of your investigation." Within moments Mason became very emotional. He said, "Joyce was my rock ...the love of my life. She was everything to me and our children. The way she died was an evil I can't describe. What a senseless loss. I could forgive those involved in her death if it weren't for fact that they took my children's mother away from them. There are no words to describe how I feel. I know those murderous scum will be punished by our law and by God's law, but it can't bring Joyce back to us. I miss her so very, very much. It is said that *time heals all wounds* and I pray it will heal mine, but it seems unbearable. Now it's up to me to live for my children. I need them and I know they need me. I've been away from them way too long. Soon …soon I will be back with them."

Colonel Hunter was pleased with his interview with Mason. There would still be military and political ramifications to deal with related to Mason's mission, but Colonel Hunter would deal with them one day at a time.

It's been three weeks since Mason (Ted) was returned to the United States. Broken and scarred from his years in prison, it's amazing that he's is still alive. He is recuperating as well as could be expected under the circumstances, and getting stronger every day. His broken ribs, legs and arm required surgery, but the doctors were optimistic that they would heal in time. His body had been covered with burns and infections that the doctors were aggressively treating. Though he had to be in tremendous pain, he didn't complain. He just said, "I just thank God that I'm alive." He will need a great deal of physical and emotional therapy. His emotional scars are as serious if not far deeper that his physical ones. Everything considered he should be well enough to go home to his family soon. Just going home will be a big step in his emotional therapy. His out-patient therapy could continue for months.

Chapter *14*

Her Death Requited,
He is at Peace

Seventeen years ago, Ted Murphy who we now know was also CIA Operative Steve Mason, was out of the military and happy to be a husband to Joyce and a father to Catherine and Christopher. He was living comfortably with his mother Alice and father Edwin in a farm house in Vestal, NY. In what seemed to be a 'split second', life as he knew it changed forever.

In the *darkness beyond the night* of January 19, 1992 Joyce's life ended. Catherine would live the next seventeen years, longing for her mother, her father and her brother. For all those years, not knowing what happened to them. Though she loved her Grandmother Alice with all her heart, there was always an unappeasable feeling of loss, an empty feeling that gnawed at her sense of well-being. Seventeen years later, life as she knew it changed again. She found Chris, the brother she hadn't seen since she was five. Because of Trent and Kassidy's recent visit, today she has found even more hope for the future.

It's been two weeks since Trent and Kassidy came to the door with their wonderful news. It's been difficult for Catherine and Grandmother Alice to contain their excitement. It's early October and the leaves are an array of gorgeous bright orange, red, and yellow colors. The air is crisp and clean and a slight breeze rustles through the leaves of the four huge Maple trees that surround the house.

This morning Catherine awoke with a smile on her face and a skip in her step. It was the weekend and she didn't have to go to work so she, Chris and Grandmother Alice had a leisurely breakfast together. They relaxed on the porch, Grandmother with her tea in her favorite chair and Catherine and Chris with their morning hot chocolate, swinging on the porch swing. As a cool breeze blew through Catherine's long silky blond hair, she thought what a great day this is, with my brother here. Chris was reading a book and Grandmother Alice was humming 'In the Garden' as she often did while relaxing in her rocking chair. After awhile, Catherine decided to go back inside. Chris followed. They both admired the beautiful fall centerpiece Grandmother Alice had placed on the coffee table in the living room like she does every year. There were fall decorations on the fireplace mantle, and in other places throughout the house that she made with flowers from her garden. She always likes to decorate the house to match the seasons. As Grandfather Edwin said, "It's always important to honor the seasons and God will bless you with abundance."

Catherine's emerald green eyes had a sparkle to them as she went into the study to play a piece on her piano. She invited Chris to join her. It was more than a release from the everyday stresses of life. She enjoyed playing the piano, and it often took her back to the pleasant days of her childhood. As she sat down to play, she thought, "My father used to do the same thing with his violin." The sun streamed through the stain-glassed window, dispersing a rainbow of colors across the piano while Catherine played 'Moonlight Sonata'. As she glanced up at the angels carved by her Great-Grandfather Edward in the woodwork over the window, she remembered her father's words of hope. He said, "I hope that the angles are watching over you and Chris just as they were on the front of your medallion." She clasped the medallion in her hands and held it close to her heart as she said a prayer of hope that her father would be able to come back to her soon.

It was late afternoon the next day and the great aroma of Grandmother's cooking in the kitchen filled the house. Just then, the doorbell rang. Catherine said, "I'll get it Grandmother." Chris was following close behind.

When Catherine opened the door, a man in a military uniform said, "I am Colonel Hunter with the United States Marines Corps, are you Catherine?" She said, "Can I help you?" He said, "I have someone out here in the car that would like to see you; …we would like to come in?" Catherine said, "Just a minute," and shouted to Grandmother, "Please come to the door I think I need you." So Grandmother came quickly to the door. Just then, Colonel Hunter helped a six foot two tall man with slightly graying hair climb the steps to the front porch. He was walking with a cane. There was a brace on both legs and a cast on his left arm.

"Hello Catherine, Mom, and is this Chris?" Catherine just stood there for a minute not knowing what to say. Grandmother Alice said, "Please come closer". She hesitated for a minute and then threw her arms around the man. With tears in her eyes she said, "Thank God, you really are Ted?" He said with tears in his eyes, "Yes mom it's me." Catherine and Chris looked stunned. Chris asked, "You're my real dad?" Ted said, "You must be Chris. Yes I'm your real dad. Then, he faced Catherine and said, "You must be Catherine." Chris asked, "How do we know you are our real dad?" There is something that you, Catherine, your grandfather and I all have in common." He asked Colonel Hunter to lift up his shirt in the back, then turned with his back towards Chris and said, "See, we all have dimples in our shoulders." Chris, Ted, Catherine and Alice all laughed a little. Chris and Catherine gave their dad a hug. Ted said, "Chris you've grown-up into a handsome looking young man, and Catherine you are more beautiful than I could have ever imagined."

Her heart still pounding like it was going to leap from her chest; Catherine took her father's hands and pulled him close. She put his hand over her heart and said, "For the first time in seventeen years dad, the emptiness in my heart is gone." Ted said, "Yes, Our family is whole again. Though your mom isn't here in person, she is in our hearts forever and we are all together at last."

The End!

ENDNOTES

1   In 1992: SUNY, Binghamton was the State University of New York located in Vestal. It is now called "Binghamton University," with a Binghamton address for enrollment purposes, but it's actual location is Vestal, New York.

2   http://www.ncis.navy.mil. About NCIS, History, Leadership, and Today's NCIS

3   http://en.wikipedia.org/wiki/Gulf War. Invasion of Kuwait, and Norman Schwarzkoph

4   Ibid.:

5   Ibid.:

6   Ibid.:

7   http://en.wikipedia.org/wiki/Gulf War. Coalition of Gulf War

8   Ibid.:

9   Ibid.:

10   Ibid.:

11   http://www.en.wikipedia.org/wiki/1983 Beirut barracks bombing.

12   http://www.en.wikipedia.org/wiki/1983 Bombing of the American Marines barracks in Beirut, 23 Oct 1983.

13   Ibid.:

14   Ibid.:

15   http://www.shrc.or/data/aspx/d7:1097.aspx. International Report on Tadmur Military Prison

16   Ibid.:

17   http://www.fbi.gob/about-us/cjis/fingerprints biometric/iafis/iafis

18   http://www.fbi.gov/CODIS Home Page, A-Z Index

19   Except for direct quotes, all characters names are fictitious